"Sixteen months ago I kissed you, and a few months later you slugged me in the jaw in Jake's Place parking lot."

Her mouth fell open, but she didn't utter a word. She didn't know what shocked her more: the fact that Eric had *again* brought up that kiss on Sunset Beach or his reference to her impassioned, impulsive act last summer…or possibly the evidence that said jaw was now hovering half a foot away from her upturned face.

"I…I've never apologized for that. I'm sorry," she whispered.

"I didn't bring it up because I was looking for an apology."

"No?" she mouthed. She stood frozen to the spot, even though she knew she should back away.

"Which do you regret more?" he asked.

When she just stared at him, her bemusement obvious, he clarified, "The punch? Or the kiss?"

For a stretched few seconds, neither spoke. The silence was absolute. Colleen wondered if they both held their breath.

Dear Reader,

Hello, and thank you for reading the latest installment of the Home to Harbor Town series! Of all the Harbor Town heroes and heroines, I feel as if I have such a fond spot for Colleen and Eric. Sometimes I could perfectly hear their snappy, sparking banter in my head. They've grappled with their attraction and seeming dislike for one another in the background of the first two Harbor Town books, so I was especially glad to give them center stage for their own opposites-attract, emotional, very passionate romance.

Colleen Kavanaugh is a woman who knows her own mind, and she's convinced the last person on the face of the earth that she'd fall for is arrogant, know-it-all playboy Dr. Eric Reyes. Eric has always resented the fact that their shared tragic history has created such a barrier between him and Colleen, and he's not above using the circumstances of their siblings' upcoming wedding as an excuse to get closer to her.

I hope you enjoy Colleen's realization that the heart can be blind, and that an avowed enemy just might offer the ideal opportunity to learn, to grow and to love with the full force of the passionate Kavanaugh spirit.

Find out more about the rest of the Home to Harbor Town series at www.bethkery.com.

Beth Kery

CLAIMING COLLEEN

BETH KERY

™ **Harlequin**®

SPECIAL EDITION

Recycling programs
for this product may
not exist in your area.

ISBN-13: 978-0-373-65659-2

CLAIMING COLLEEN

Copyright © 2012 by Beth Kery

www.Harlequin.com

Printed in U.S.A.

Books by Beth Kery

Harlequin Special Edition

The Hometown Hero Returns #2112
*Liam's Perfect Woman #2136
*Claiming Colleen #2177

*Home to Harbor Town

Other titles by Beth Kery available in ebook format.

BETH KERY

holds a doctorate in the behavioral sciences and enjoys incorporating what she's learned about human nature into her stories. To date she has published more than a dozen novels and short stories, and she writes in multiple genres, always with the overarching theme of passionate, emotional romance. To find out about upcoming books in the Harbor Town series, visit Beth at her website, www.BethKery.com, or join her for a chat at her reader group, www.groups.yahoo.com/group/BethKery.

I'd like to thank my editor, Susan Litman, for having faith in these stories and for her excellent suggestions in crafting and content. Lea, thank you as always for your generosity and valuable feedback. My heartfelt appreciation goes out to my husband, who manages never to tire of my frantic schedule and who always seems to offer the exact kind of support I need.

Prologue

Sixteen months ago

The spring evening was unseasonably hot and humid, but the remnants of winter still lingered in Lake Michigan. Colleen Kavanaugh Sinclair shivered for the first five minutes of her swim, but by the time her internal clock told her it was time to turn back toward shore, the cool water felt delicious sliding against her heated skin.

Her swim off Sunset Beach was as much a part of her summertime routine as taking her children, Brendan and Jenny, to soccer or baseball practice. Traditionally, her first swim of the season happened on this weekend. But this Memorial Day would be her last swim here. This evening, she was saying goodbye to Sunset Beach.

She climbed onto the sand and dried off, thinking of all the times she'd cavorted on this beach with her brothers and sister while their mother, Brigit, sunbathed and chatted with her friends. The late-night bonfires and holiday barbecues. Her sister's water-skiing events—never again.

Colleen had acquired her final memory tonight. Her favorite public beach had been gobbled up by the wealthy elites of Harbor Town. She'd personally gone and spoken out against the privatization of the public park at the last few city council meetings, but in the end, money talked louder than she could.

Movement caught the corner of her eye. She turned and saw *him* standing there.

"It's a nice night," Eric Reyes said, his voice low.

Colleen froze in the action of toweling off her bare belly, caught off guard by his bare-footed, silent approach in the sand. His dark eyes flickered downward, making her skin tickle with sudden awareness.

She knew who he was, of course.

He'd already finished high school by the time Colleen and Liam attended Harbor Town High. She'd known who he was before that, though. He'd worked for the local landscaper. More than once, the tall, dark boy with the serious expression had caught the attention of Colleen and her friends when they saw him working shirtless in the park or unloading a truck on Main Street. She'd heard once through the grapevine that he was Harbor Town High School's best hockey player.

Eric Reyes wasn't like Colleen, or Mari Itani, or any of her other friends who vacationed with their families in Harbor Town during the summers. He was a year-rounder who worked and who didn't have the time to while away the hours on one of the beaches in the charming lakeside vacation community.

One summer before the accident—she couldn't recall which summer, precisely—Colleen had been walking with several of her girlfriends down Elm Street and saw Eric Reyes coming out of the Harbor Town Library, several books in the crook of his arm. He'd paused on the sidewalk, probably struck by the gaggle of suntanned teenage girls. Her friends had grown predictably giddy in the vicinity of a good-looking, older boy, but when Colleen's eyes met his, she'd given him a smile.

Now they stood face-to-face again, strangers who shared a past. Fifteen years ago, her father had killed his mother in a three-way car crash. The lawsuits against Derry's estate had drastically altered the Kavanaughs' economic status. Eric had used his portion of the lawsuit to go to medical school. Now he owned a luxurious Buena Vista beachfront home, and she was the trespasser on the familiar beach.

Now *she* was the outsider.

Seeing him standing there caused anger to flare hot inside her, the strength of it shocking her a little.

"Are you going to call the police?" she asked him quietly.

"I hadn't planned on it, no. Why, are you about to do something illegal?"

She had a wild urge to manually remove that little smirk he wore.

"It's illegal for me to *be* here. I never saw you at any of the city council meetings, but surely you know about Sunset Beach becoming private."

"I know about it."

"Yeah. I thought so." She unfastened the band at her neck and began to work a comb through her hair. "I can't imagine *you* wanting the beach to remain open to the great unwashed." She glanced at him in annoyance when he chuckled. He raised his dark brows when he noticed her scowl.

"You look pretty clean to me." His gaze once again flickered down over her bikini-clad body. She stiffened. It didn't offend her, his glance, or creep her out like some men's stares had in the past. It *did* unsettle her.

Bedroom eyes.

The phrase leapt into her brain unbidden. Dark eyes… knowing eyes. It surprised her a little, to feel this strong sexual current emanating from him. How dare he, given their past, look at her with such potent male appreciation? So what if practically every female in Harbor County would have patiently waited in a mile-long line to be on the receiving end of a sultry gaze from single, gorgeous Dr. Eric Reyes? Not every female in Harbor County shared the same messy, tragic history with him that Colleen did.

She stepped closer and tilted her chin in a subtle challenge. "You never did answer me. Did you vote 'yes' for the homeowners taking over Sunset Beach, or not?"

"Of course I voted for it. It was an excellent investment. I would have been a fool to turn down the opportunity."

She gave a soft bark of laughter and stepped away, shoving her things into her bag, her rapid, abrupt movements betraying her swelling agitation. She felt weak...vulnerable... unable to control her reaction. The realization sent her already frothing emotions into a boil. Words poured out of her throat against her will.

"That's the only thing you thought of when the opportunity arose? What about the townspeople? What about the local kids who take swimming lessons off Sunset? All you thought about was the investment? The *money?* Don't you have enough of that, Reyes?"

"You know what they say. You can never have too much."

Her long hair fell in her face when she jerked her head up and glared at him. The slant of his mouth told her he was angry...maybe as angry as she was. He'd been provoking her.

He'd succeeded.

Never one to back down from a dare, Colleen dropped her bag back on the beach and stepped toward him. "You came out here to taunt me."

Something flashed in his eyes, an emotion she couldn't quite identify. "You're wrong."

"Am I? You didn't come out here to throw it in my face?

This beach wasn't just one more thing you can take from a Kavanaugh? This isn't your victory lap?"

He shook his head slowly. "You really are a little princess."

Her heart started to pound out a warning in her ears. She stepped closer, her jaw clenched hard. "What's that supposed to mean?"

"You didn't know that's what the guys used to call you? Little Princess Kavanaugh. Well, I'm real sorry if I knocked off your crown."

"How dare you say something like that to me," she breathed out through a constricted throat.

"Seems to me you dare worse, only you don't seem to mind if your insults are based on ignorance."

She was *so* furious—so agitated—her consciousness went hazy. Maybe it was because her heart was charging like an out-of-control locomotive, but the world took on a surreal cast. When she turned jerkily to retrieve her items from the beach, she stumbled and nearly did a face-plant on the sand.

Eric caught her left upper arm, then steadied her further by grasping her right. She tried to jerk out of his hold, made a little wild by boiling emotion.

"Colleen, stop it. *Please*."

His voice barely penetrated her chaotic emotions. She couldn't believe this was happening to her. The explosion of feeling had come out of nowhere.

Or maybe it hadn't.

Maybe it'd been brewing since the night she'd gotten that phone call while she was at camp when she was sixteen years old. Maybe this cyclone of feeling started to coalesce when she'd learned her father was dead, as were three other people he'd crashed into while he'd been driving drunk.

She heaved again, trying desperately to break his hold on her, but he was every bit as strong and fit as he appeared. Instead of releasing her, he cursed beneath his breath and turned her toward him, now holding her securely by her shoulders. Distantly, she realized her cheeks were wet with tears. Humiliation surged through her. She hated that he was staring at her with those concerned, knowing eyes, seeing the evidence of her vulnerability.

"Let go of me," she grated out.

But as her feet faltered in the soft sand yet again, he brought her closer to his body, attempting to steady both of them at once.

"You're going to hurt one or both of us. Just calm down," he said, his voice low, but resonant with emotion.

His warm breath struck her from above, whisking across her right temple. She went still in sudden awareness. His arms were around her, her breasts were plastered against his chest. His heat penetrated though his clothing and emanated into her damp, naked skin. Her eyes widened when she felt his body harden against her, as if he'd become aware of her at the precise moment she'd become aware of him.

"Colleen?"

She blinked. His quiet voice had felt like a caress.

She wanted to look up into his face at that moment…open herself to him…just a crack.

The realization made her start to struggle again, this time with increased force. Her heart bounded in her chest as if in a panic to escape her rib cage. She caught him off guard after her moment of stillness. He cursed—loudly this time—when she forced him off balance. They both went down on the beach, a surprised *oomph* escaping her throat at the impact of her hip hitting the sugar-soft sand.

"Are you okay?" he asked anxiously.

"I…I…yes, I'm fine." The abrupt fall seemed to have popped the anger right out of her, leaving her stunned and breathless.

She stared into his face. He sprawled over her body, his elbows in the sand. He felt large and hard, covering her with plenty to spare. She couldn't comprehend how his eyes could be so dark and yet blaze so hot.

The moment stretched like a live wire drawn taut.

Colleen didn't know how it happened—had he leaned down, or had she strained toward him?—but suddenly his mouth was on hers, his lips firm and demanding. Hungry.

Everything transformed in a split second. Need rose in her with the strength of a striking talon. She tangled her fingers in his hair and scraped his scalp with her fingernails. He groaned low in his throat and slanted his mouth at a different angle, his kiss somehow tender and ravishing at once. The tip of his tongue slid along the seam of her lips.

She parted her lips and slid her tongue against his, arching her back into him, this time of her own volition, compelled by sudden, driving desire. The hardness of his chest was such a welcome relief to the aching tips of her breasts. She pressed down on his back, desperate for more of the sensation of him. Heat seared her from the inside out, softening her, filling her...thawing her.

She gasped in dazed disapproval when the pressure of his mouth disappeared. Eyelids heavy, she met his gaze. He stared down at her, his facial muscles rigid, his nostrils slightly flared. He looked exactly like what he was: a virile male primed to stake his claim. Part of her longed for him to do just that.

The other part saw the question in his eyes. His bewilderment struck her like ice water splashing on her heated face.

She shoved him away. Reality must have hit him at the same moment, because she didn't have to push very hard. He rolled off her. Colleen found herself panting softly and staring up at a lavender-blue sky.

For a full ten seconds, she just lay there, her body vibrating with shock and the remnants of blazing arousal.

It couldn't have happened.

She touched her lips with her fingertips. They felt damp

and slightly swollen. She sat up abruptly at the undeniable evidence that she hadn't been under the influence of a bizarre hallucination.

Eric lay on his back in the sand, staring blankly up at the darkening sky. He looked like she felt—as if someone had just taken a swing at his head with a two-by-four. He didn't move, but his gaze flickered over her. His eyes focused when they found her face. They softened.

Two thoughts soared into her brain, the first causing anguish, the second panic.

She hadn't felt desire that powerful, that imperative, since Darin had died.

No. She'd *never* felt anything like that.

She scrambled up from the beach.

"Colleen!"

She grabbed her shorts and hurriedly stepped into them, nearly falling over again in the process. She refused to look at him, but out of the periphery of her vision she realized he'd sat up and was watching her.

"Colleen," he repeated. "Don't leave. Talk to me."

Her heart felt enlarged, like it was pressing too tight against her breastbone. Unwanted tears blurred her vision. What was wrong with her? She'd just kissed Eric Reyes like her life depended on it. Now his deep, low voice coaxed her in the twilight.

"Just…just leave me alone," she said haltingly—stupidly—before she yanked her T-shirt over her head.

He picked up her tote bag, holding it out to her like a peace offering. "I didn't come out here to ask you to leave. I've watched you swim here the last few summers. I came out here tonight to tell you to continue."

Her head swung around, and their gazes locked. She wished like hell she didn't believe him. His kindness was too much to bear after that sudden upsurge of grief and anger followed by that inexplicable blaze of pure desire. A wild need to escape overwhelmed her.

Tears blurred her vision as she grabbed her tote bag and jogged across the sand, leaving the source of her turmoil behind.

Chapter One

The first thing Colleen Kavanaugh Sinclair saw when she walked into Dr. Fielding's familiar examination room was her son, Brendan, slouching in a chair. The second thing was her arch-nemesis standing nonchalantly next to him. Once she took in Eric Reyes's unexpected presence, pretty much everything faded from her awareness for two stunned seconds.

Of course, he wasn't really her arch-nemesis. That was just stupid. An enemy would have to mean something to her, and Eric Reyes did *not* mean anything.

"Colleen, Dr. Reyes mentioned that you two know one another." Dr. Fielding's voice interrupted her dazed disbelief.

She blinked and forced her attention to Dr. Fielding. He looked especially short, round and amiable while standing next to the brooding, dark tower of maleness that was Eric Reyes. Dr. Fielding had moved to Harbor Town around twelve years ago, soon after Colleen herself had returned. He'd delivered Brendan and her daughter, Jenny. Because he hadn't lived in Harbor Town at the time of the crash, he clearly didn't get the history and thick emotion that ran like a humming electrical wire beneath his seemingly innocuous statement about her and Eric knowing one another.

"Did he?" Colleen returned, eyebrows arched.

"Yes, he's told me you two work together at The Family Center. Wonderful place. I've heard Colleen speak twice now about the facility," he said, turning to Eric. "Once for the Rotary Club and once for the Pediatric Society in Detroit. She's a talented public educator and speaker, in addition to being a gifted clinician. But I'm sure I'm not telling you anything you don't know, Eric," Dr. Fielding said.

His warm, friendly glance between Eric and Colleen melted when he noticed Eric's wooden expression and Colleen's averted gaze. She inhaled deeply for courage. If Eric could seem so calm, so could she.

"*I* work at The Family Center," Colleen corrected. "Dr. Reyes is a volunteer. He comes in a few hours a week." *Blessing us with his supreme presence,* Colleen finished silently. Eric's mouth twitched, as if she'd spoken the words out loud. If she hadn't been thrown so off balance by Eric's unexpected presence at her son's doctor's appointment, she probably would have had to hide a grin at the knowledge that her arrow had hit its target.

"What are you doing here?" she asked him quietly instead.

Eric held up a chart. "Dr. Fielding consulted with me about Brendan's case today. I examined Brendan. Even though your son hasn't quite finished his course of penicillin, I recommended an X-ray and bone scan. We've received the results."

"*You* recommended them?" Colleen repeated. She hadn't realized he'd examined her son, although she now recalled Brendan mentioning a *funny, cool young doctor dude* who had looked at his foot last week before Colleen had taken him for X-rays in a different part of the hospital. Dr. Fielding had said he'd have a specialist take a look at the foot, but neither that comment or her son's description had brought to mind

Eric Reyes, who, in Colleen's opinion, was an interfering, arrogant block of ice. Sure, he might have that glossy, dark, movie-star-quality hair and angular jaw that kept the secretaries at The Family Center wide-eyed and breathless. And she conceded he possessed an authoritative yet trustworthy bedside manner.

But Colleen's days of being overwhelmed by those surface charms were long over.

"Dr. Reyes is Harbor Town Memorial's finest orthopedic surgeon, Colleen. I immediately went to him when I had questions about Brendan's foot problem."

Her brow crinkled. She glanced anxiously at Brendan. Her son gave a small, sheepish shrug and rolled his eyes. Her heart squeezed in her chest in compassion for him. She knew how much he longed to be back playing football, how much he despised all these doctor appointments. The "foot problem" had become the bane of his twelve-year-old existence.

Over the past month, Brendan had acquired a limp. Initially, it'd hardly been noticeable, but it became more pronounced every day. Brendan denied any serious pain, insisting there was only a dull ache in his right foot. Colleen had assumed he'd pulled a muscle or gotten run over by an unusually big kid at Little League football practice, although Brendan and his coach insisted nothing out of the ordinary had occurred. She'd made an appointment with Dr. Fielding, not really expecting anything more than the normal bruises and sprains Brendan had acquired over his active boyhood years. Dr. Fielding had discovered internal swelling and recommended a course of antibiotic treatment. Much to Brendan's distress, Dr. Fielding had also put the kibosh on any more football for the rest of the season.

Eric Reyes was an orthopedic surgeon, though. His presence at this day-long hospital visit implied the foot problem was a good deal more significant than a bruise or infection.

"He needs a specialist? It's that serious?" Colleen asked Eric.

"Brendan hasn't responded to the course of oral antibiotics. The swelling of the soft tissue has increased, as has his pain. Considerably," Eric replied.

She knew patients at The Family Center responded to Eric to an uncommon degree, seeming to instinctively trust his intelligent, incisive, perpetually unruffled manner. What he was saying in that even, authoritative tone didn't soothe Colleen at the moment, however. It frightened her.

This *did* sound serious.

"Your pain is worse?" Colleen said, turning to Brendan. Her son shrugged again.

"It doesn't hurt that bad," Brendan mumbled.

"On a pediatric scale of pain, Brendan is scoring in the high category," Eric said.

"Brendan, why didn't you tell me you were hurting so much?" Colleen asked worriedly. Brendan hunched down, revealing little to her but the crown of his dark gold, wavy hair. She forced down a maternal desire to go over and hug him. She swore her son had skipped preadolescence and moved right into teenage rebellion. It bewildered her at times, how independent he wanted to be, how withdrawn he could get. One second he'd been an adorable, chubby two-year-old, the next he'd become an impenetrable puzzle.

Colleen wasn't ready for her little boy to grow up. She wasn't prepared to deal with Eric Reyes. She wasn't ready for any of this.

"Some people are underreporters of pain," Eric said, diverting her attention away from Brendan. He approached her and opened the medical chart. "It's actually fairly common among active, athletically inclined kids. Brendan's not being dishonest when he says it doesn't hurt that bad. He just has a high pain tolerance, that's all."

She glanced up quickly into his face. Typically, she made

a point of not standing so close to him when they worked together at the Center. At five foot eight inches, she was tall for a woman. Her brothers were both tall men, but in general, she wasn't used to having to look up so far into a man's face. She especially hated having to do it with Eric.

He showed her the contents of the folder, pointing at an X-ray. "Here's the problem. Do you see this dark portion here? That's an osteolytic lesion at the first metatarsal of Brendan's foot. It's beginning to punch into the bone."

"*Lesion?* Wait…you don't mean—" Colleen stopped herself short, her mouth hanging open. She gaped at Eric as the beginnings of panic started to roil around in her belly. The word she'd stopped herself from saying in Brendan's presence echoed around in her skull like a ricocheting bullet.

Cancer.

"It means that the inflammation of the soft tissue is starting to eat away at a portion of Brendan's bone," Eric said quietly. She stared up at him, unable to look away from his eyes. The compassion she saw in them couldn't penetrate her alarm. Neither did Dr. Fielding's reassuring touch on her upper arm.

"Dr. Reyes is recommending surgery on the foot, Colleen," Dr. Fielding said in his warm, grandfatherly manner. "I'd like to admit Brendan this afternoon. We've already briefed him, and Dr. Reyes has generously made room in his schedule. He'll be able to do the surgery first thing tomorrow morning."

"No," Colleen blurted out.

"Uh…*no?*" Dr. Fielding repeated, confused. "Colleen, this is my recommended course of treatment. Dr. Reyes feels the surgery should be done as soon as possible, and I agree wholeheartedly. "

"May I talk to you for a moment? In private?" Colleen asked Eric in a high-pitched voice.

She distantly noticed through her rising anxiety that Eric

looked much calmer than Dr. Fielding, almost as if he'd expected Colleen's reaction. He nodded toward the door.

She gave Brendan a reassuring smile and brushed back his bangs. "I'll be right back. Okay?" She waited for her son's nod before she followed Eric. He led her down the hallway to a dark, empty exam room.

"What do you mean, *lesion?*" she demanded the second he flipped on a light and closed the door. "What is it, exactly, that's eating into Brendan's bone?"

"It's likely that some kind of foreign body somehow managed to lodge itself in the tissue. I questioned Brendan about it. He does recall stepping on a good-sized thorn when he was at the beach months back."

"But—"

He held up his hand in a "pause" gesture.

"I know he probably never said anything about it to you. He wasn't aware that something had lodged in his foot. I won't know more until I can get in there and clean up the tissue."

"But you said *lesion.* You said something was eating away at the bone. Does that mean it's cancerous?"

The edges of her vision darkened, as if just saying the word out loud had taken everything out of her. Eric stood just inches away, one hand on her upper arm, steadying her. When had he moved closer? Colleen wondered dazedly.

"No, no, it's not cancerous," he said hastily. "It's an unusual situation. The cells are irregular, yes, because of the persistent inflammation. The location of the lesion is isolated, though. A minor surgery and debridement of the tissue will take care of things completely. On the other hand, we shouldn't wait, because the health and structure of Brendan's bone is at risk. I wouldn't want it to develop into osteomyelitis. He'll get an intravenous cocktail of antibiotics, but that's the only postoperative treatment he'll require besides some physical therapy. We'll follow him closely afterward, but there's every reason to believe that a cleanup of the tissue and removal of the foreign body will resolve things."

Colleen stared blankly at the light blue shirt he wore beneath his blue lab coat. "The bone hasn't been damaged permanently?"

"No," he replied, his firm tone reassuring her despite her disorientation.

"I want another opinion."

"I thought you might say that." She glanced up. A shock went through her when she finally took in how close he was to her. He'd combed his hair back, but the long bangs had fallen forward and brushed his cheekbone. A five o'clock shadow darkened his lean jaw. He had a cleft in his chin. She didn't know how it was possible that his midnight eyes could be as cold and hard as onyx at times, and so warm at others.

Like now.

"The only other orthopedic surgeon at Harbor Town Memorial is Marissa Shraeven." He leaned his head to the side and hitched his chin toward Brendan's chart, keeping his gaze on her the whole time. Colleen realized he'd tossed the chart on the exam table before he'd reached out to steady her. "I had her review the case. She agrees one hundred percent with my course of treatment."

The pressure of his hand increased subtly. She turned out of his hold and took several steps, distancing herself. His nearness was only increasing her unrest.

"I'd like Dr. Shraeven to operate, then."

"Really?" he asked dryly.

She spun around. "What's that mean?" He looked so calm that for a split second, she was sure she'd misunderstood the edge of sarcasm in his tone. He reached and retrieved Brendan's chart.

"I think you know what it means," he said mildly, his gaze flickering over the chart.

"I just don't think it's appropriate for you to operate on Brendan."

"Are you questioning my ability?" he asked, looking up.

"No." She gave an exasperated sigh when he merely quirked up one brow in a challenging gesture.

"My integrity, then?"

"I'm not questioning your ability or integrity. I just think that given everything…given our pasts, there has to be a better option."

For several seconds they just stared at one another while Colleen listened to her heartbeat drum loudly in her ears.

"So you're falling back on the excuse of the crash, is that it?" he finally said.

"Does it surprise you? My father killed your mother sixteen years ago in a car wreck. I know how you feel about the Kavanaughs. I know how you feel about me," she finished under her breath.

"Do you?"

She hoped her incredulous glance reminded him of it all—the deaths of their parents, his sister's considerable injuries and facial scarring, the lawsuits brought against Colleen's father's estate by the Reyes and Itani families, their silent battle of wills while the two of them worked together at The Family Center…

"I'm not buying it," he said.

"Excuse me?"

"I'm not buying that you don't want me to operate on your son because your father killed my mother in a case of reckless homicide."

"Oh, really? You can think of a better reason why I wouldn't want you to operate on Brendan?"

"I can," he said quietly, glancing up from the chart. "Sunset Beach, Memorial Day weekend, last summer."

His image swam in her vision. She breathed through her

nose slowly, trying to calm herself. Her knees went weak. She felt flattened and numb at once.

She couldn't *believe* he'd just mentioned that night so casually. They'd worked together at The Family Center now for over a year—distantly and infrequently, granted—but still, they'd seen one another, spoken to each other…

…simmered in each other's presence.

Never once during that time period had he acknowledged what had happened on the beach that hot, early summer night. Colleen had been all too eager to comply with his silence on the matter. She'd never been able to come to terms with that kiss; never could logically make sense of it. It shocked her to the core that he'd just brought up that forbidden topic in this situation. She'd long known Eric Reyes had nerves of steel, but she'd underestimated him.

His cockiness was titanium strength.

"I'm the most qualified orthopedic surgeon in Southern Michigan," he continued. "Are you really going to waste precious time booking appointments with other specialists who are going to tell you exactly what I just did? All because you're too proud to acknowledge a kiss? Or are you too stubborn to admit how much you liked it?" he added in a low, rough voice.

He'd done the impossible for the second time in her life. He'd made her hyperaware of her weakness, not to mention speechless with the knowledge. She responded precisely as she had that first time on Sunset Beach.

By turning and walking away.

Late the next morning, Colleen and her mother conferred across the hospital bed, their voices hushed because Brendan lay sleeping between them. He'd awakened in the recovery room earlier, but he'd soon fallen asleep once he'd been hooked up for his first round of IV antibiotics. To Colleen, he looked smaller than usual lying motionless in that bed, more vulnerable than she cared to consider with the tubes running from his arm to the machine administering the medication.

"I wish Dr. Fielding would come and examine him," Brigit Kavanaugh said as she studied her grandson, her brow creased with worry.

Colleen experienced a twinge of annoyance at her mother's uncertainty about Eric Reyes operating on Brendan. Guilt followed her mild irritation. What right did she have to be annoyed at her mother when she'd expressed even worse doubts about him just yesterday afternoon?

It hadn't taken her long to work past her wariness about Eric. Of course she wanted the most qualified surgeon available. Brendan's well-being was her top priority, and if that meant she had to squirm in discomfort because of the identity of the most qualified candidate, so be it. She heard from practically everyone on the planet how skilled, smart and gifted Eric was at his job. Working with him for the past year plus had proven to her the accolades weren't overrated. He was talented, all right, even if his approach with her patients had occasionally set her on edge. He'd been known to trump her clinical opinion a time or two.

But truth be told, Eric's kindness and attention both toward Colleen and Brendan before and after the surgery had cooled her uncertainties considerably.

"Brendan is under Dr. Reyes's care, Mom," she said quietly. "He says the surgery couldn't have gone any better. He assured me the wound has been completely cleaned. Brendan is going to be fine."

Colleen waited, her breath burning in her lungs, sure she knew what her mother would say next. *He's only a* specialist *because he took all of our money in that lawsuit and bought himself a medical degree.* She'd learned to dread her mother's hurt and defensiveness every time the crash or anything relating to it was mentioned.

But the bitter words never came.

Brigit had changed a lot in the last two months, ever since Liam—Colleen's brother—had confronted her about her past; ever since old Kavanaugh family secrets had been exposed, secrets that revealed why Derry Kavanaugh had been so upset and intoxicated on that fateful night sixteen years ago. The Kavanaugh family was still reeling from the revelation of those painful truths, perhaps Brigit—the secret-keeper— most of all.

Brigit had not only hidden the fact that her daughter Deidre was another man's child for Deidre's entire childhood, she'd also withheld the identity of Deidre's father until just a few months ago.

At times like this, Colleen found herself missing her mother's anger. It was better than the quiet, sad resignation that seemed to have replaced the bitterness.

"I know, but still…Dr. Fielding delivered Brendan. He knew Darin," Brigit added, referring to Colleen's husband, who had died in a special operation in Afghanistan three years ago. Brigit gently tucked the blanket around Brendan's waist. "We've known Dr. Fielding for so long now."

They'd known Eric Reyes longer, Colleen thought. Her mother hardly needed reminding of that, though. One of the innocent victims of the crash had been Eric Reyes's mother, Miriam. Another victim had been his sister, Natalie. Natalie had escaped the tragedy with her life, but she'd spent the better part of her eleventh year in the hospital, suffering from severe injuries and scarring sustained in the accident. Eric had been both father and mother to his little sister since he was eighteen years old.

It was no wonder Eric could be so cool and businesslike at times, Colleen admitted to herself. He'd hardly ever had the opportunity to be a carefree teenager. None of the kids in the Itani, Kavanaugh or Reyes families had really had much of an opportunity for that. At least, not since the crash.

She stood like she'd bounced off springs when the object

of her thoughts walked into the room. She was surprised to see him so soon after he'd conferred with her so extensively postoperatively only around an hour ago. He was so tall that he seemed to fill up the small, curtained-off area of the hospital room completely. Or maybe it wasn't just his physical stature that caused her reaction, but the strength of his formidable personality.

He nodded at Colleen in a friendly, professional way.

"Out like a light, huh?" he murmured as he studied his patient.

"He's been asleep for about forty-five minutes. Should I wake him?" Colleen asked.

"No, he's fine. The nurse took his vitals before he fell asleep, and he looks likes he's resting easy. I'll come back in a bit and check on him."

Colleen nodded. She had a feeling that most surgeons didn't offer this much bedside attention, and she was thankful.

She was also a little confused by his solicitation, but she thought she might understand it. Colleen had worked as a social worker in hospitals for most of her adult life. She was familiar with the professional courtesy employees in the medical field extended one another when it came to caring for family members. Besides, thanks to Liam and Natalie's flourishing romance, Eric and Colleen were related now, in a sense. Colleen had managed to deny that connection in her mind for the past several months as she watched her brother and Eric's sister growing closer and closer. It seemed impossible to ignore it under these new circumstances, however.

"Mrs. Kavanaugh," Eric said politely to her mother, "are you comfortable? Would you like something to drink?"

Color stained her mother's pale cheeks. She wondered if it was the first time Eric and her mother had met with anything less than animosity since the courtroom proceedings following the crash. She couldn't help but feel thankful to him for his kindness.

"I'm fine," Brigit said softly, her gaze averted. "Thank you for taking such good care of my grandson."

"He's a strong kid. Smart, too. I had nature on my side as his doctor." He glanced at Colleen. "I'll just come back in a short while."

"Thanks," Colleen said.

She hadn't meant for the word to come out sounding so pressured...so earnest. Maybe it was his unexpected kindness toward her mother that had made her sound that way. His gaze flickered over her face, and his small smile faded. Their gazes locked. For a split second, she was unguarded. She felt it: that connection that took place whenever she looked—really *looked*—into his eyes. For the first time, she admitted that jolt of awareness was the reason she'd been so determined to avoid his presence for over a year.

She glanced away, feeling breathless.

"Of course," she heard him say stiffly before he left the room.

Her mother picked up a magazine and began to leaf through the pages. Colleen suspected she was trying to be tactful by not discussing Eric. What did one say, precisely, in these unusual circumstances?

The silence stretched, interrupted only by the soft beeps of the IV machine and the distant sound of voices at the nurses' station. She had nothing to distract her from recalling that charged glance she'd shared with Eric before he'd left the hospital room just now. She couldn't seem to stop herself from remembering other things, as well...things she'd rather stayed buried, feelings she found highly disrespectful and unsettling, given her love for her husband.

She didn't want to remember. Not when her son had just had a surgery.

Not *ever*.

Her undisciplined thoughts kept veering into forbidden territory, however. She couldn't seem to stop herself from recalling every detail of what had happened on Sunset Beach nearly a year and a half ago. Surely her memory was playing tricks on her.

There was no way Eric's body could have felt so hard or fit against her so perfectly. No man alive could possibly taste so good.

Ridiculous. Impossible, Colleen assured herself heatedly. It was some strange combination of their argument and their volatile history that had made the moment so electric.

The noise of her mother setting her magazine back on the bedside table started Colleen out of her memories and ruminations.

She sighed and brushed her son's bangs off his forehead. Brendan still slept. He'd never let her pet him like this if he was awake, she thought, a familiar small pain going through her.

She hadn't set a toe on Sunset Beach for over a year now, despite Eric's invitation to continue with her swimming routine. She'd been all too happy to forget that bizarre, inexplicable incident. Kissing Eric just didn't fit in to her safe, known world. When Eric appeared just as eager as she was to ignore what had happened, Colleen had assumed he was as regretful as she was.

So why had he made a point of reminding her of it yesterday in that examination room?

Even if they didn't share a turbulent past, he was the exact type of man Colleen disliked: opinionated, arrogant, bullheaded. Movie-star-caliber good looks could only get a guy so far when they were accompanied by all those less-than-stellar qualities.

Besides, hadn't her father used to say Colleen had cornered the market on stubbornness in the Kavanaugh family? It was no wonder she didn't get along with Eric. They were like repelling magnets. Was that why her heart give a flutter when she heard someone enter the hospital room? She breathed a sigh of relief when she saw the tall man who appeared next to the drawn curtain wasn't the handsome surgeon.

"Hey," she greeted quietly, smiling at her brother, Liam. He was in uniform, and his wavy, light brown hair streaked with gold looked windblown. "Did you walk over from the station?" The Municipal Building, where Liam worked as the chief of police, was only a few blocks from the hospital complex.

"Yeah, sorry I couldn't get away sooner. How's he doing?" Liam asked in a hushed tone as he bent down to give his mother a kiss on the cheek.

"He's doing great," Colleen replied. "Eric says the wound looks clean and that the bone tissue should heal with time. Brendan's going to have to do some physical therapy, though."

"That shouldn't be too much of a problem. It'd be more of a challenge to keep Brendan still for any extended period," Liam said, grinning. "Did Eric say what had lodged in his foot?"

"A rose thorn, of all things," Brigit murmured, shaking her head.

It struck her as a little surreal to hear her little brother say Eric's name so casually. A year ago, he would have said *Reyes* with a hard edge to his voice and a frosty look in his blue eyes. Now he spoke of him as he would a close friend or family member. Which Eric was, in a way, Colleen conceded. Liam had told her point-blank last month he'd fallen hard for Eric's sister, Natalie.

Still, the change in the landscape of her life disoriented her a little. Things had seemed much more comprehensible when Eric Reyes was her enemy, pure and simple.

No matter. Brendan would be out of the hospital in a few days, and she and Eric could go back to keeping their wary distance from one another.

Liam sat down, and they talked for a few minutes in hushed tones until they were interrupted by the nurse coming in with a pitcher and some plastic cups.

"Dr. Reyes says he can have ice water when he wakes up if he wants it," the nurse told Colleen.

Brendan's eyelids flickered at the sound of the nurse's voice.

"Mom?" he asked hoarsely, sounding a little anxious and disoriented. Colleen placed her hand on his forearm and squeezed gently.

"I'm right here, honey," she soothed.

He focused on her sitting next to his bedside, and his anxiety immediately vanished. "I'm thirsty," he said.

"Perfect timing, kid," Liam said as Brigit stood to pour him some water. Brendan turned his head on the pillow and returned his uncle's grin groggily.

"How are you feeling, Brendan?" Brigit asked.

"Okay."

"Your foot doesn't hurt?" she asked. As if her words had reminded him, Brendan lifted his head and stared down at his bandaged foot. He groaned, and his head fall back on the pillow.

"Does that mean yes?" Colleen asked anxiously.

"It doesn't hurt, Mom," Brendan assured, meeting her eyes.

Colleen loved her son to the ends of the world at the moment. He got exasperated with her mom-worry sometimes, but deep down, he knew how much she loved him.

"He just saw the bandages and thought of all the boring hours of lying in bed," Liam said knowingly.

"Dr. Reyes said I can start moving around later this afternoon. He says it'll make my foot stronger," Brendan told Liam between sips of water.

"Did someone say my name?" Eric asked. The curtained-off portion of the already small space suddenly seemed as crowded as a dorm-room party.

"Hi," Brendan said, smiling at Eric. "Did you do a good job on my foot?"

"Your mom didn't tell you?" Eric asked.

"I just woke up," Brendan said, leading Colleen to believe he didn't remember much about his groggy transfer from the recovery room to his hospital bed.

"Then I'll tell you," Eric said. "You're going to be tackling your uncle here by Thanksgiving, because I did a *fantastic* job."

Brendan gave a tired little whoop of celebration.

Colleen couldn't help but give a grudging smile as she watched Eric and Liam shake hands in greeting. She had to hand it to him. His cockiness was only exceeded by his charm.

Brigit and Liam stepped out of the room to give Eric room to examine Brendan, giving Colleen a chance to observe Eric's easy banter with her son and the way Brendan seemed so comfortable with him.

"Do you work with kids a lot?" Colleen mused after he'd finished Brendan's nerve response test, joking and talking with her son and distracting him with the fact that he was gently poking at his exposed toes with a sharp-looking metal instrument.

"I did my residency in pediatric orthopedic surgery," Eric said. "When I was hired at Harbor Town Memorial, it was with an understanding that I'd be serving both adults and children, though."

"Why did you decide to come back to Harbor Town when you could have worked in a larger hospital and just focused on children?" Colleen asked, puzzled. It suddenly struck her that she really knew absolutely nothing about him. Eric opened his mouth to respond but was interrupted.

"Hi, Brendan. Hey, Colleen." Colleen looked around to

see Natalie Reyes, Eric's sister, peering around the curtain hesitantly. Eric glanced at Natalie and then back at Colleen. Suddenly, Colleen had her answer. He'd sacrificed some of his personal goals because he'd felt a fraternal responsibility toward his younger sister.

Natalie must have come from her office, because she wore an attractive chocolate-brown suit that highlighted her svelte figure and dark eyes.

"Should I come back later?" she asked.

"No, I'm all finished. My patient gets perfect marks," Eric said. He walked over and gave his sister a peck on the cheek. Colleen noticed that Brendan's eyes went wide at the gesture. He looked stunned that his newly acquired friend had just done something as treasonous as kiss his uncle's girl right in front of him. Eric must have noticed, because he grinned.

"Natalie is my sister, Brendan." He threw Colleen a quick, wry glance. "I see no one told you that, either."

"Well, I'm sorry! It never came up. We were thinking about other things, like emergency surgeries," Colleen said defensively.

"Natalie is your *sister?*" Brendan asked.

Natalie smiled and nodded.

"Didn't the same last name ring any bells?" Eric asked, chuckling at Brendan's continued wide-eyed stare of amazement.

Brendan grinned and shook his head.

"Liam told me you're doing really well, Brendan," Natalie said.

"I'm okay. Just sleepy," Brendan said before he grimaced slightly. "And a little…"

"What?" Colleen asked.

"Sick to your stomach?" Eric asked from behind her.

"A little," Brendan admitted.

Colleen glanced around at Eric. He obviously read her concern, because he gave her a small smile.

"It's normal to be groggy and a little nauseous after the anesthesia. I'll have the nurse bring in some soda and crackers. Then Brendan can take a nice long nap."

Natalie walked out of the room with her brother while Colleen stayed with Brendan, who was having trouble keeping his eyes open. Eric returned a few minutes later. He hadn't just told a nurse to bring something to soothe Brendan's stomach. He'd brought the items himself.

"I really didn't expect you to do all this," Colleen said in a hushed tone as she stared at Brendan's sleeping face. He had drunk half a cup of soda and eaten two crackers. He'd said his stomach felt better before he'd promptly fallen asleep.

"Why do you sound so surprised?"

Colleen blinked and turned around from where she was sitting at the edge of Brendan's bed. She'd been surprised, all right—by the nearness of Eric's quiet, gruff voice, not by his solicitation. He stood a foot or so behind her. Her face was at the level of his abdomen. Her gaze flickered up the length of his scrubs. His eyes gleamed in his shadowed face as he looked down at her. She found it impossible to break his stare. The moment stretched.

Her heart seemed to stall in her chest as he reached to touch her cheek.

Chapter Two

"Is he sleeping?" a woman whispered from behind them. Colleen started out of her trance, feeling like she'd been caught in an illicit act, which was ridiculous. She self-consciously brushed at her cheek with her fingertips, feeling nothing but her heated skin. There must be something there, though. Surely Eric had just been about to innocently remove some dust or dirt from her face.

Natalie peered at them next to the drawn curtain. Something about the hopeful, hesitant expression on her delicate features made Colleen forget her unease.

"Yes," Colleen replied.

"I...I was wondering if Liam and I could speak to you two?" Natalie asked.

She glanced up at Eric, who looked just as confused as Colleen felt, then back at Natalie. "Us? Together?"

Natalie nodded. "Maybe we can talk down in the waiting room at the end of the hall? There's something important we'd like to discuss with both of you," she whispered, a trembling smile on her lips. Colleen couldn't quite interpret her expression. Was it excitement? Or anxiety?

"Sure," Colleen said more confidently than she felt. She turned to Brigit, who had just re-entered the room. "Mom, could you stay with Brendan while we run down to the waiting area? I could use a soda. I'll be back in just a bit."

Brigit agreed, and Colleen, Natalie and Eric filed out of the room. When they reached the waiting area, she saw Liam was the only other occupant. Natalie sat next to him, and Eric and Colleen took seats just across from the couple.

"We could do this another time if you're *uninterested,* Eric," Natalie said, her mouth settling into a grim line that didn't at all match her lovely, delicate features. Looking at Eric, Colleen realized his expression had turned cold. Hard. As she glanced back and forth between their stubborn faces, Colleen realized just how much brother and sister resembled one another. Two identical pairs of eyes shot sparks back and forth.

What the heck? Colleen thought. She'd only really gotten to know Natalie over the last several months, but she'd never once seen her any way but even-tempered and pleasant. Leave it to Eric to be the one to instigate this unlikely reaction in a paragon of virtue like Natalie. Still…why had Natalie's suggestion about their meeting turned Eric into a glaring block of ice?

"I didn't say I was uninterested," Eric said.

"Fine," Natalie replied, her eyebrows still arched in a challenge.

Colleen didn't get what was going on here, but she had a long history with brothers. Marc and Liam were fantastic, but she and her sister, Deidre, had learned long ago the importance of banding together in the face of male arrogance. Eric remained turned in profile to her, but she could almost feel his disapproval like a cold breeze. Yes, *this* was the Eric

Reyes she knew—the man who had turned brooding into an art form.

"Anybody want a soda?" Liam asked, standing.

"What did you want to talk to us about?" Colleen asked Liam immediately once he'd handed them their drinks and sat down again.

"We were going to take you two to lunch separately—someplace nice—to break the news, but then Brendan got admitted into the hospital and our plans had to be changed. I suggested we get in the squad car, turn on the sirens and use the bullhorn to spread the news to everyone in Harbor Town, but Natalie wouldn't let me. Spoilsport."

"Liam," Natalie remonstrated with a smile and a slap on his arm that turned into a caress. They both were glowing. Liam stared at Natalie, grinning, and suddenly they were kissing.

"Wait," Colleen said, the truth slowly dawning. "You two aren't... You're not..."

"We're getting married," Liam said in a perfunctory manner before he leaned down to kiss Natalie again.

Natalie's laugh before she was silenced by Liam's kiss was clear and musical, the very sound of happiness. Colleen just sat there holding her unopened can of soda, dumbfounded.

"But you haven't even known each other for four months now," she said, even though Liam and Natalie looked far too busy to be listening.

"Not even three," Eric corrected morosely from beside her.

Colleen did give him a quelling glance that time. He lifted one raven-dark brow and levelly returned her sardonic stare. The fact that he could look as handsome as the devil when he was being such a jerk really steamed her.

In truth, she felt torn. The last thing she wanted to do was agree with Eric on something—anything—but she *did* feel that Liam and Natalie were being rash. Surely it was too soon in their relationship to decide on marriage. She and Darin had engaged in a whirlwind love affair before they'd married. They'd been young and foolish, and wild to be together before he was deployed to the Persian Gulf for his first tour of duty. Colleen wouldn't have changed that decision for anything, given the way things had turned out, but at this point in her life, she recognized they hadn't exactly behaved wisely.

Then there was the news of what she'd learned about her own parents several months ago. She'd always assumed her parents were the ideal couple. She'd considered their marriage inviolate. Recent events had proved her wrong.

In a gut-punching type of way.

Brigit and Derry Kavanaugh had each engaged in an extramarital affair in the early stages of their marriage. Colleen's sister, Deidre, was in truth her half sister. Finding out that Deidre wasn't his biological daughter was what had instigated Derry's extreme distress and intoxication on the night of the crash that had changed their lives forever.

Yes, Colleen was a bit jaded on the concept of marriage at the moment.

"So, you plan on a long engagement, Liam?" Colleen asked. "The two of you should have plenty of time to be sure about—"

Liam lifted his head and spoke, interrupting her. "We're getting married December 14. We've already booked the date at Holy Name. We took the first day we could get." He gave Natalie one last kiss, this one quick and tender, before he leaned back and took a swig of his soda. Both of them were grinning from ear to ear.

"It'll be a Christmas wedding," Natalie said to Colleen.

Since Natalie had started seeing Liam, she didn't hide as much behind the dark glasses that helped to protect her light-sensitive eye. The glasses also covered the scars on her left temple—scars she'd received in the accident as a child. At the moment, the lighting in the waiting room was dim enough that Natalie wasn't wearing her glasses. There might never have been a devastating car wreck sixteen years ago if Natalie's shining eyes and joyous expression were any indication.

"*Christmas*. But it's already almost Halloween," Colleen exclaimed.

"We can't wait a day longer," Liam said.

Natalie leaned forward, looking concerned. "I know it's probably a bit of a surprise. But Liam and I could really use both of your support and help in this. We don't want a large wedding, but there will be a great deal to organize, I suppose."

"I'll do whatever I can do to help, of course," Colleen said, all the while feeling guilty about the fact that she was harboring reservations about the quickness of this decision. Liam was courageous—true—but his boldness bordered on impulsivity at times. He'd been known to volunteer for the most dangerous assignments when he'd been a Chicago police detective. Not that marrying Natalie was the same as a risky assignment, but still...

"Are you sure?" Liam asked her. "You knocked yourself out with the planning for Mari and Marc's wedding, Colleen. Ours won't be as fancy. We just want family and good friends." He grinned. "And a great party, of course."

Natalie was studying her brother. "You haven't said anything, Eric."

"I don't think it should come as a shock to you that I think you two are jumping the gun on this," Eric replied bluntly.

A tense silence ensued. Colleen squirmed uncomfortably in her chair. She agreed with Eric, but she hated the sadness that seeped into Natalie's radiant expression and the way Liam's grin flattened.

"I want to make it clear, we're not asking for permission," Liam stated after a moment. "Or for approval," Liam added, meeting Eric's stare. "Natalie and I *are* getting married. I'm crazy about her, and I want to take care of her for the rest

of my life, be there for her…love her." He glanced over at
Natalie, and the glow of love flared once again in her dark
eyes. "Some people take years to know whether or not they
want to make that commitment. Natalie and I have known
since this summer." Liam glanced from Colleen and back to
Eric. "Believe or don't believe. Just know that Natalie and
I *do* believe in each other…in this." He took Natalie's hand
in his and faced them again. "If that's good enough for you,
we'd like both of you to be in the wedding, too."

Despite her anxiety over the situation, Colleen couldn't
ignore the love and determination, the pure joy, in his tone.

She stood and rushed over to him, hugging him tight and
offering her congratulations. Natalie came next. Colleen
kissed her on the cheek.

"I'm finally going to have a sister who lives here in town,"
she said before she gave Natalie a hug.

"I'm finally going to have a sister, period," Natalie replied,
laughing.

Over Natalie's shoulder, she noticed Eric still sat. Colleen
hitched her chin slightly at Natalie in a pointed gesture, glaring at him the whole time.

*Get off your butt this instant and congratulate your sister,
Reyes.*

His hard mouth twitched—probably in annoyance, because it couldn't possibly have been in humor, given the situation—and he stepped toward his sister.

"You're sure?" he asked simply.

"I am. I love Liam so much," Natalie replied before she
flew into her brother's arms.

"I just want you to be happy." Colleen blinked back a tear
when she heard the deep feeling infused into Eric's usually
level voice.

"I've never been so happy in my life," Natalie said.

Liam's smile was unusually tender when Colleen met his
stare. She realized her face was damp with tears. When she

glanced back at Eric and Natalie, she saw that Eric watched her as well over Natalie's head, his eyes dark and inexplicable.

Later that afternoon, Eric called out to Colleen as she was walking out of the hospital gift shop.

"Did they take Brendan down to the physical-therapy gym?" he asked as he caught up with her. He couldn't help but notice how her expression became guarded when she recognized him. Every time he told himself he was used to her defensiveness and dislike, that it really didn't matter, Colleen surprised him.

It mattered.

She nodded. "It seems strange to have him moving around right after surgery."

"Don't worry. The physical therapists here are real pros. They'll just be assessing him and doing some simple stretches to keep his muscles flexible and strong. I'm glad I caught up with you. Can we talk in my office?" he asked as they progressed down the hallway together.

Her bluish green eyes flashed. "Why?"

"Liam and Natalie."

"I can't believe they're getting married," she murmured.

"That's what I want to talk to you about."

"What do you mean?"

He held out his arm, beckoning her down a corridor to the right of them. "My office is down here. Please?"

She wore a pair of supple black leather boots that hugged her shapely calves just as tightly as her form-fitting jeans hugged her thighs. Colleen didn't look like the mother of any kid he'd ever operated on before, but that wasn't saying much. Colleen made a habit of breaking most stereotypes, even if she could be rather predictable when it came to certain things.

Like hating him, for instance.

"What's wrong? Not afraid of being alone with me, are you?" he teased softly when he noticed her wavering in those sexy black boots.

"Don't be ridiculous. Let's make it quick, though. I want to get back before Brendan's appointment is over." She strode down the hallway, her boot heels clicking briskly. Per her typical MO, she left him standing there like a gawping teenager stunned into immobility by her golden beauty.

Fortunately, he wasn't a teenager anymore. He did what any red-blooded man would have done under the circumstances and stood still, admiring the rear view of Colleen Kavanaugh Sinclair in a pair of tight jeans. She came to a halt and turned her head, the abrupt gesture causing her mane of long blond hair to whip around her.

"Are you coming or what, Reyes?"

He knew she didn't expect an answer, just compliance, so he said nothing as he caught up to her. Neither of them spoke as they walked side by side down the hospital corridor to his office.

He'd known her since he was seventeen years old—or at least, he'd known *of* her. They hadn't exactly moved in the same social circle. She was a Kavanaugh, after all, and he was the son of an immigrant who cleaned Harbor Town offices and hotel rooms. She was a daughter of a wealthy Chicago attorney who could afford to buy a vacation home in Harbor Town and provide his wife and children with sunny, perfect vacations that lasted not just for two weeks but entire summers. Colleen had been the prettiest girl in a group of very pretty girls. She'd been the best athlete, the bravest and the smartest of that elite group, as well.

Some people couldn't help it. They were born having it all.

Of course, appearances could be misleading. Tragedy had struck Colleen not just once, but twice by the time she was thirty years old. First her father had been killed in the wreck when she was sixteen. Then her husband had been killed in Afghanistan several years ago.

He knew that for most men, the first things that would pop into their head when they considered Colleen was her good looks and effortless ability to talk to anyone. It was why she was such a talented clinical social worker, after all. She could put a long-term drug addict and recidivist criminal at ease as quickly as she could a wealthy blue blood who was struggling with his wife's alcoholism. Eric knew that Colleen was probably born with a lion's share of kindness and charm, but it was her pain and grief that had molded her into the person she was today.

Of course, he only knew about her kindness and natural ability to connect with other people from observing her during her clinical work. That, and the memory of a bluish green-eyed stare and a smile that could haunt a man for half a lifetime.

Sometimes he was convinced that he couldn't stand Colleen when she turned on her Princess of the Icy Realm act, but his irritation at her was usually only short-lived. He understood that their uneasy history sparked her hostility, and she did it to defend against past hurt. Once he got some distance from her, his annoyance at her would become tinged with sadness.

He'd watched her work, and the truth was, he admired her. She was no pushover, and the patients at The Family Center knew better than to try to manipulate her. Her kindness wasn't of the "sweet" variety, but the deep, enduring, measurable type; it was demonstrated daily through her relentless faith in people's ability to heal and her track record for going the extra mile for her patients—not occasionally but as a matter of course.

It sucked, plain and simple, knowing he was one of the few people on the planet who couldn't make Colleen smile. He wished he hadn't been forced into admiring and respecting her from a distance. He'd rather be doing it up close and personal.

"I'm right in here," he said.

She followed him into his office. He sat on the edge of his desk and observed her while she glanced around curiously and then wandered over to his bookcase, smiling when she saw a photo of a ten-year-old Natalie. Nat wore a tutu and an anxious, hopeful smile. Colleen took a few steps and looked closely at his diplomas, and then his old hockey stick from college. She sobered when she saw the photo of his mother.

There it was.

For the thousandth time, he wished the weight of the past didn't stand like a ten-foot-thick barrier between them.

"They say that men who are so neat have something to hide," she said briskly as she turned around. She sat down in one of the chairs in front of his desk and crossed those long, booted legs.

"Who are *they*, exactly?"

"Okay. *I* say that," she replied with a bewitching little smile.

"I thought women liked a man who picked up after himself."

"Maybe some women." Her eyes flickered over him briefly before she glanced out the window at the brilliantly sunny fall day. For a moment, he took pleasure in examining her while his regard went unnoticed. Her heart-shaped face managed to convey delicate, feminine beauty and strength all at once. She wore her bangs long and spiky. They highlighted her large, expressive eyes to perfection. Her hair was loosely curled and tumbled around her upper arms and back, and as always, he experienced a desire to delve his fingers into those glossy locks.

"So, what did you want to talk to me about?" she prompted.

He cleared his throat and forced himself to focus.

"I was watching you in the waiting room when Liam and Natalie announced they were getting married. I saw your expression. I know I'm not the only one who thinks they're being impulsive about this."

Colleen shrugged. "I didn't make a secret of it. My brother is a wonderful man. He'll make Natalie very happy. You've got nothing to complain about."

"And you do?"

She stood up quickly. "Not at all. I happen to like Natalie very much."

"I like Liam, as well. I *do*," he said when she gave him an incredulous glance. "Granted, I haven't always. But he's gone out of his way to get to know me over the past few months. I know that hasn't been easy for him, either. I respect the fact that he's done it for Natalie's sake. He's not the first person I'd pick for Nat, but—believe it or not—he's not the last," he admitted gruffly.

"Stop. Your benevolence is overpowering me."

"Cut the sarcasm for a second, will you? I'm trying to talk to you about something serious. You can listen to everyone else on the damn planet. Can't you do it with me for ten minutes?"

She froze. He hadn't intended to sound so sharp. Regret swept through him when he saw the color fade from her cheeks. He closed his eyes briefly and took a deep breath.

"I care about my sister, and I know you feel the same for Liam. Would it be so awful for us to both think they're rushing into this marriage? Would it really be so terrible for us to share an opinion on something?"

She glanced away from him. He guessed he'd irritated her, but he sensed she was torn, as well.

"You know what I mean, Colleen," he continued in a low voice. "Even though you don't want to admit it, you think they're making this decision rashly. You don't want to see Liam get hurt any more than I want to see Nat suffer."

She said nothing as she stared out the window. Despite her cold expression, he knew if he touched her smooth cheek, she'd be warm.

And soft.

He stood and walked around his desk, moving away from her because he had a sudden desire to move closer. His movement put him in her line of vision. He caught her eye.

"You know I'm right," he said quietly.

She looked annoyed. "Why do you always have to make a habit of proving that point?"

He shrugged and fell into his desk chair. He stretched and placed his hands behind his head. She glanced down over his neck and chest. He went still in sudden awareness.

She looked abruptly out the window. "There's nothing we can do. They've made up their minds. You know how impossible it can be to talk reason to two people who are drunk in love with each other."

"We have nearly two months to make them pause and reconsider their hastiness in the matter."

Her eyes flashed at him. *"We?"* she asked, looking haughty—and damn beautiful. He nodded soberly, trying to prove to himself he was affected by neither of those things. He had a lot of experience, at this point, in deflecting Colleen's burning stares.

Her beauty was a lot more difficult to ignore.

"Look, Marc and Mari will also be in the wedding party," he said, referring to Colleen's brother and his wife. "But you and I live here in Harbor Town. We'll hire a wedding planner, but we'll probably be the relatives most involved in the preparations."

"And you're reminding me of these unfortunate circumstances *because*…"

"Because it will give us a chance to…tweak the situation a little. Maybe provide Liam and Natalie with some more realistic perspectives on just how serious the venture of marriage is, and encourage them to take some time and at least think about extending their engagement."

She stared at him, then shook her head slowly. "You've got real nerve, you know that, Reyes?"

He smiled.

Color rushed into her cheeks. "It wasn't a compliment," she snapped.

He shrugged, hiding his grin with effort. Even when she snarled at him, she appealed. "Either way, you must realize what I'm saying makes sense. It's not just Natalie I'm thinking of here. It's Liam, too."

She narrowed her eyes. "Do *not* try and make it seem like you're being generous. It's weakening your case. Considerably." She began to pace in front of his desk. "Even if I did agree with you that they're being impulsive, there's nothing we can do. I know it won't make any difference for me to talk to Liam about it. He's stubborn as an ox when he makes up his mind about something, a Kavanaugh through and through." She looked up. "Can you talk to Natalie?"

"I've tried a dozen times. It's like talking to steel armor. The Kavanaughs haven't cornered the market on stubbornness," he said mildly.

"Humph," she muttered, her sweeping gaze telling him loud and clear that while she doubted his claim in his sweet sister's case, she certainly believed he'd received his fair share of bullheadedness. "What exactly do you mean by 'tweaking the circumstances'? Do you want me to reveal some deep, dark secret about Liam to Natalie? Should I tell her that he used to not change the empty toilet-paper roll when he was fourteen years old? Do you think that will send her running?"

"No," he replied levelly, refusing to allow her to prick his temper. "But I can think of a few things that might cause one of them to hit the pause button if the information was presented in just the right way."

"Like what?' she asked suspiciously.

"Don't give me that look. I'm not picturing anything traumatic. Do you think I would ever purposefully hurt my sister?"

She hesitated, but when she finally resumed pacing and answered, she sounded honest enough.

"No."

"Thanks for the vote of confidence," he said, forcing himself to look away from the distracting sight of her scissoring thighs.

She rolled her eyes. "Are you going to tell me what you have in mind or not?"

"It's simple enough. We just make sure Liam and Natalie encounter the type of thing that would make any rational person stop and consider before leaping impulsively into marriage."

"What? Force them to watch old documentaries about failed celebrity marriages? Remind them repeatedly of how much Brad said he adored Jennifer before Angelina woke him up?"

"No. But not too far from that. Has it ever occurred to you that we're mutually acquainted with couples who have gone from head over heels to heading to divorce court in record time?"

She paused and studied him. He leaned back in his desk chair, musing.

"It might be...*prudent* for Liam and Natalie to observe some of those jaded couples firsthand. We can start off by asking a few of them to the engagement party," he said.

"I beg your pardon?" she asked, her forearms crossed beneath firm, generous breasts.

Definitely not *like the typical mother of his patients.*

"The engagement party you and I will be throwing Liam and Natalie," he said reasonably. "We should plan to have it as soon as possible. Maybe even next weekend, given the short period of time we have before the wedding."

He pretended to misunderstand her incredulous—or was it horrified?—expression.

"Sorry. I just assumed.... Somebody is going to have to throw them an engagement party, and we're the most likely candidates. Don't you want to? I thought that was the right thing to do."

"I...of course, it's..." She made a sound of frustration. "Don't tell me what the 'right' thing to do is, Reyes. Who made you the leading authority on correct wedding etiquette?"

"I'm far from being an expert. That's why I need your help so much," he said as humbly as possible. He rocked back in his chair, thinking. "I want my sister to have the best of everything. She deserves that, and more. But I really believe they should consider hitting the slow-down button before taking the big plunge."

"Maybe," Colleen muttered after a moment of silently wearing down his carpet with her treading feet. "But I'm not agreeing to anything malicious. If they're determined to get married after only knowing each other a few months, there's absolutely nothing anyone can do to change their minds."

"I agree one hundred percent," he said. "It's not meant to be hurtful. Just...a wake-up call."

"Other than that, we'll give them a *wonderful* party."

"Are you kidding? We'll throw them the best engagement party Harbor Town has ever seen. The best wedding and reception, as well."

She stood directly in front of him, her jean-covered thighs slightly spread. "Do you promise that's the only thing you'll do? Try to subtly encourage them to extend their engagement? Because I'm not agreeing to anything dishonest."

"I promise. I despise dishonesty," he said truthfully.

He waited while she studied him closely.

"Okay," she finally conceded. "Mari, Marc, you and I will be responsible for the cost and planning of the engagement party. As for the wedding and reception, can you speak with Natalie and get some of her thoughts on decorations, budget, that sort of thing? I'll do the same with Liam, just so we're all operating on a consistent plan."

He nodded. "I understand the bride's family is traditionally responsible for the finances. I'm Natalie's whole family, so I'll be paying for the wedding."

She paused, her mouth hanging open.

"That's very generous of you to offer," she said slowly after a moment. He couldn't decide if he should be flattered or insulted by her expression of surprise and grudging respect at his offer. "But couples finance their weddings a lot of different ways these days, and I'm sure Natalie would agree you're under no obligation. Plus, I doubt Liam would ever expect you to pay for everything, but that's something we have to clarify."

"I agree," Eric said.

She nodded once firmly, despite her doubtful expression. "I'll see you later then."

"Let's have lunch tomorrow," he declared when she started to walk out of his office.

"Why?" she asked, spinning around.

"To plan the engagement party. And, of course, how we implement our ideas for promoting careful consideration instead of impulsive haste with Natalie and Liam."

Her eyes flickered over him warily.

"What's bothering you?" he asked.

"Nothing. It's just…I had no idea you were such a cynic when it came to the idea of true love, Reyes. I suppose I should have suspected it."

"I like to think of myself as a realist, not a cynic. Besides, you've admitted you agreed about this. Committing to another person for a lifetime requires some serious contemplation. There's no such thing as love at first sight. Right?"

"Of course not," she said, bristling.

"So, what's your excuse?"

"What do you mean?"

"Your excuse for being a cynic when it comes to hasty marriage?"

A shadow fell over her features, and he immediately regretted his words. He'd just been trying to get to know her better. Instead, he'd unintentionally struck a bad chord, Eric realized. Colleen had been burned by romance in the past. Maybe she was still sensitive because her husband, Darin Sinclair, had been killed in action.

"I am not a cynic," she said stiffly. "I just think Liam and Natalie need more time to make sure this is what they truly want."

He struggled to get back on the right track again. "So, we're on for tomorrow at lunch?"

"All right. I guess that'll work," she said. He lowered his hands and sat forward in his chair when he noticed her further hesitation.

"What is it, Colleen?"

"It's nothing. It's just…are you certain Brendan will be okay?"

He exhaled slowly to give himself a few seconds. Seeing Colleen vulnerable wasn't something he was used to, so he hadn't adequately prepared himself for the experience.

"He's not just going to be okay," he said. "He's going to be great. I'm even more confident in saying that now that I've seen how well the tissue cleaned up. I know you won't take my word for it, but time will prove my case."

A smile flickered across her lips; just the hint of it had him longing to see its full, blazing glory.

"I do trust you…about Brendan," she added softly before she walked out of his office.

Eric leaned back again and brought up his feet on his desk, his gaze fixed on the door that had just closed behind her. He'd told her he hated liars, and it'd been the truth. Eric didn't like subterfuge and was only planning a few reality checks in the midst of these wedding plans because he cared about Natalie so much. Other than that, he'd do everything in his power to give his little sister a wedding that would make every woman in Harbor County green with envy.

Despite the fact that he disapproved of Natalie's quick wedding plans, he found himself anticipating having a good excuse to spend time with Colleen. He didn't think that qualified him as a liar, necessarily, because he hadn't revealed that morsel of information to her. If he had, she wouldn't have consented to work with him on the wedding in a million years.

There was something about Colleen. He wanted her, and it was stupid to deny it. He considered himself to be too levelheaded to give in to the Kavanaugh-inspired hysteria that seemed to have affected his friend Mari along with Natalie. He liked women, though…some more than others. Colleen appealed to him.

A lot.

She was a challenge, and he always rose to a challenge, no matter how long he had to wait or how much planning was involved. Given the door of opportunity that had just opened before him, he couldn't pass up the chance to get closer to the stubborn, gorgeous woman who had just stalked out of his office.

Chapter Three

Colleen watched her son hobbling down the hospital hallway on crutches, chattering the whole time with the young man who was his physical therapist. After the surgery, he'd been fatigued. This morning Brendan was energetic, curious about the goings-on in the hospital, and asking Colleen, his grandmother, the nurses and Eric every question a healthy twelve-year-old boy could concoct in his active brain.

Brigit had brought Colleen's daughter, Jenny, to visit her brother before school. It'd been the best kind of maternal medicine in the world to hear her two children conversing animatedly or asking the nurse funny questions about the use of this or that piece of medical equipment or mutually grossing out when they received an honest answer. Colleen was so relieved to see Brendan's returned vibrancy it was like a physical weight had lifted off her.

Her relief didn't seem to be preventing her from experiencing a nervous, fluttery feeling that had been mounting every hour as their lunchtime meeting approached.

Ridiculous.

"I've made a to-do list," Eric said from behind her. Colleen started, his presence taking her by surprise and jangling her already rattled nerves. "Since I haven't got the slightest idea how to plan for an engagement party, let alone a wedding, I never really got past the title on the page."

Colleen regarded the man who was responsible for the butterflies in her belly. He'd left his lab coat in the office and was wearing a pair of dark blue trousers and a crisp blue-and-white-striped button-down. The pants fit his long legs and trim hips perfectly. She ran her gaze over the considerable length of him and hid her appreciation at what she saw. He was *too* handsome. She cocked an eyebrow. "You're going to be a real helper in all this, aren't you?"

His flashed a grin that struck her as extremely sexy.

"I promise not to be a hindrance, if that's any conciliation."

She gave a doubtful snort, and they started down the hallway. Two nurses twittered a greeting at Eric as they passed a nurses' station. Colleen rolled her eyes when she noticed the women's warm smiles and continued stares as they trailed Eric's progress down the hall.

"Part of your fan club?" she murmured through a small smile.

His dark brows furrowed before he glanced over his shoulder. "I work with them," he said, as if the four words automatically explained those covetous female glances.

"Uh-huh," Colleen smirked. "So, where are we going for lunch?"

"The Captain and Crew?"

She shook her head. "Emilio's?"

"Sultan's?"

She gave him a surprised glance followed by a small nod of respect. "You got it."

"I wouldn't have pegged you a lover of Middle Eastern cuisine," Colleen mused several minutes later as she tore apart a honey-drenched, nutty roll and popped some of the delicious confection into her mouth. The cozy, sunlit restaurant and bakery was doing a decent business, but they'd managed to snag the last empty booth.

"Sultan's is my favorite restaurant in town."

"Really? It's my favorite, too," she added before she could censor herself.

"I keep telling you that you really don't know anything about me," he said as he stirred his aromatic coffee. His tone sounded deceptively casual. She paused in the action of sucking the honey off her forefinger and glanced into his face. He regarded her silently, one of his arms sprawled across the back of the booth, his eyes gleaming in an otherwise impassive face…his gaze narrowed on the finger in her mouth.

Flustered, Colleen reverted to using her napkin.

"Every time you've ordered food for the staff at The Family Center, you've ordered from Bistro Campagne," she said, referring to what was arguably the nicest restaurant in Harbor County.

"And so you came to the conclusion that I'm a snob, is that it?" he said, taking a sip of his coffee.

"I never said that," Colleen replied defensively, even though she had difficulty meeting his stare. She'd never spoken her thoughts out loud, but she actually *had* been annoyed when Eric had ordered expensive catered luncheons during special occasions and holidays. It always seemed to smack of patronization—the great Dr. Reyes lavishing the little people with a treat to liven up their small lives.

He made a scoffing noise. She scowled at him. She *really* did dislike him at times. So why was it they seemed to have the ability to read each other's minds so effortlessly?

"I arranged the luncheons through Bistro Campagne because my housekeeper also happens to do catering events there, so it's easy. I give her dates and some vague details, and she turns my request into something that makes me look like I know what I'm doing." He gave her a pointed glance. "With *most* people that's what happens, anyway."

Luckily, the waiter chose that moment to arrive with their entrées, and Colleen was spared having to defend herself. She eyed his fragrant plate of steaming chicken tagine with frank interest.

"Want some?" he asked, sounding amused.

"Maybe in a bit," she said, unrolling the napkin around her silverware. Her fattoush salad with shrimp looked equally delicious. She removed a notebook from her bag and opened it to a page where she'd already started to jot down some notes. "Okay. Time to get this show on the road."

Eric's eyebrows rose as he watched her take a bite of salad and then grab her pen in a businesslike manner.

"Anything you say, Captain."

She gave him a droll look as she swallowed. "Right. Just so you know, Liam, Natalie and I spoke last night and agreed on a theme for the wedding."

"Theme," Eric repeated flatly.

"Yes. Our theme is a Lake Michigan Christmas." She noticed his bemused expression. "You know...like a nautical and holiday theme combined. They both like to sail and swim, they are going to live together next to the lake...and the wedding is near Christmas. What?" she asked with a touch of asperity when he continued to stare at her like she'd been speaking another language.

"I had no idea weddings had themes. I thought themes were reserved for English 101."

Colleen groaned. He laughed. "Hey, I'm at your service. At least I have a checkbook available to provide said wedding theme. If it's what Natalie wants, she's got it," he said.

Colleen smiled and shook her head. "Well, that's something."

"It's a big thing."

"It's a big thing," she conceded. Liam and Eric had sat down together last night and come to a compromise about financing the wedding. Colleen hadn't been around during what would undoubtedly become known in family history as an infamous meeting, but she'd spoken on the phone with Liam this morning. He'd sounded irritated when he talked about Eric's insistence about footing the bill, but there'd been a grudging respect in her brother's voice, as well.

Colleen shared in that admiration. Eric might be arrogant, but he was generous to a fault, especially when it came to his sister.

"Okay. First on the agenda—announcing the engagement."

"Who else do we have to tell?"

"All of our relatives and friends. I've already contacted the *Herald,* the *Southwestern* and the *Chicago Tribune* about an announcement," Colleen said as she made checks on the paper with administrative precision.

Eric set his fork down slowly. "You have? You really do work fast."

"We have a wedding to plan in two months' time. Working fast is the entire point, Reyes."

"Huh," he muttered thoughtfully. "At what point in the next two months are you going to start calling me by my first name?"

She looked up from her pad of paper. He was grinning. He had a very handsome mouth. Shapely, but firm. Decisive. *Don't even consider that cleft in his chin.*

For a second, she recalled in graphic detail what those lips felt like moving over hers, coaxing…ravishing….

She snapped her fingers around her clutched pen. "Focus," she muttered to herself.

"I'll need you to contact the hospital-community newspaper and give them this announcement," she said, sliding a typed piece of paper across the table toward him. "I'll need a list of family members and friends you want to invite to the engagement party, and a separate one for the wedding…"

She continued briskly with her ideas and instructions, Eric occasionally nodding somberly like he wanted her to believe everything she said was sacred dogma. She wasn't buying it for a second.

"…so we've decided on a date. If you have time after lunch, we ought to be able to run over to Scrivener's to pick out some invitations for the engagement party," Colleen concluded a few minutes later, still writing rapidly in her notebook.

She tossed down her pen and took a big bite of her salad.

"Don't you think we ought to get Liam's and Natalie's opinions on the invitations?"

"No. When I spoke with them last night, they told me this engagement party is pretty much just our deal. Mari and Marc will come in to help with all the last-minute details next Thursday, and of course my mom will help out. I'm thinking of a sophisticated party, but intimate and comfortable, as well…warm fall colors, candlelight, champagne and hors d'oeuvres that really stick to your ribs versus the dainty variety. So, now that we've decided on the date and time, we just need to decide on the location."

Eric blinked and sat back in the booth.

"What?" Colleen asked, pausing in the action of stabbing her fork into a piece of shrimp.

"You're amazing."

She laughed and pointed her shrimp at him. "That's *not* what you were thinking."

"Oh, yeah? What was I thinking?"

"That I'm a steamroller."

His low, rough laughter caused the back of her neck to prickle in awareness.

"You're pretty good at that," he said.

"Steamrolling?"

He pushed his plate back and placed his elbows on the table, leaning toward her. "No. Reading my mind. So what am I thinking now?"

Her eyes widened slightly when they met his. She saw humor in their depths...and heat.

She looked away.

"We should hurry. Brendan will be getting back to his room soon, and we still have to pick out invitations," she said before she took a large gulp of ice water.

"I was *actually* thinking—among other things—about where we should have this little soiree," he stated, ignoring her attempt at changing the subject.

Heat flooded her cheeks. His small smile told her he knew precisely what she'd *thought* he'd been thinking.

"What about having the party at my place? There's plenty of space, and I have that large deck and a half-dozen heat lamps to keep it warm," Eric suggested.

"No."

His expression hardened. *One second, all easy playboy-doctor charm; the next, as arrogant as a prince.*

"Why not?" he demanded.

Colleen thought of how to respond while she chewed. She couldn't just tell him point-blank that something about his luxurious Buena Vista home on Sunset Beach put her on edge. It seemed a constant reminder of the past, the crash, the drastic change in both the Kavanaughs' and Reyeses' circumstances.

She couldn't tell him that her cursed Kavanaugh pride was responsible.

"It's large, all right. Maybe *too* large," Colleen said. "The party should be a little more intimate."

"We could rent out a room at the Captain and Crew, or Bistro Campagne, I guess," Eric mumbled, even though the scowl that shadowed his mouth said he still wasn't thrilled with the way she'd shot down his first suggestion.

"Too expensive. We all don't have your bank roll, Reyes." She saw his eyes spark in further irritation, so she spoke before he could rebut her. "What about at my place? I know it's not Buena Vista Drive, but I enjoy entertaining there. It's large enough for a party, but intimate and comfortable, as well."

"Where do you live?" he asked slowly.

"On Sandcastle Lane."

"How long have you lived there?"

She thought while she chewed and swallowed. "A couple of years now."

"So, you and the kids moved there after your husband died?"

"The house on Fifth Street was too large for just the three of us," she replied. She wasn't normally uncomfortable talking about Darin, but something about doing so with Eric made her stomach flutter nervously. In order to sidetrack him from pursuing the topic, she eyed his chicken tagine speculatively.

"Go on," he said dryly, shoving his half-eaten lunch toward her. She skewered a piece of succulent chicken, popped it into her mouth and made a sound of appreciation. Eric chuckled. She grinned while she chewed.

"Never one to hold back, are you?" he mused. "Just as passionate about your likes as you are your dislikes. I admire that."

Colleen paused in her chewing and swallowed. She set down her fork and wiped her mouth with her napkin.

"Thanks." She took a sip of water, a smile lingering on her mouth.

"What?" Eric asked, his sharp eyes noticing her repressed grin.

"Nothing," Colleen murmured. He continued to stare at her, one eyebrow cocked in a query. "It's just that you praise my passionate temperament in such a cool, levelheaded manner."

"So you think I'm cold? Dispassionate?" he stated more than asked.

Yet again, she blushed. His seemingly bland questions had brought to mind that kiss on Sunset Beach.

No. She was far from thinking Eric was cold.

"I wouldn't say you're cold. Just…analytical. That's just the impression I've gotten in your work at The Family Center." When she noticed his scowl, she added quickly, "I'm not complaining. I've had reason to be thankful my son possesses a surgeon with such a precise, logical brain." She was increasingly feeling the need to escape when he didn't say anything, just continued to pin her with a stare that made her want to squirm. She checked her watch.

"Speaking of Brendan, we better get going if we still want to pick out the invitations."

"You don't really believe I'm a walking robot, do you?" he asked.

Her eyes widened slightly. Damn. Had he read her mind *again?*

On one occasion last year, Eric had taken over the job of The Family Center's regular physician while Dr. McIntosh was on vacation. Eric had refused to fill an anti-anxiety medication for Barney Glendan, a patient of Colleen's with a concurrent history of substance abuse and panic disorder. Eric insisted the pill was mildly habit-forming. Colleen had gone to battle with him. Eric had never once lost his calm. His methodical explanation of why he wouldn't prescribe the medication had infuriated Colleen. Barney had been on the medication for years to good result and had remained sober just as long. She'd told Eric in no uncertain terms that his medical decision was completely counterproductive to the patient's health given his history of sobriety and compliance. She'd contacted Dr. McIntosh and had him fill the prescription, much to Eric's irritation. Colleen had stood firm, however. Nobody, not even the brilliant Eric Reyes, stood in the way of her patients' well-being. Later, as she'd driven home, she *had* called him an insufferable, arrogant robot.

But, of course, Eric didn't need to know that.

She closed her notebook and shoved it along with her pen into her purse.

"I do *not* think you're a robot. Some people are ruled by logic, some by their emotions. That hardly makes you a robot," she said crisply.

"Uh-huh," he muttered, his tone leading her to believe he knew he was being placated. He swiped the check from beneath her fingers when she grabbed for it. "The thing that really bothers you—"

"I never said I was bothered by anything—"

"—isn't that I'm analytic or cold," he continued, ignoring her defense and tossing some bills on the table. "It's that you recognize we're a lot alike."

Colleen snorted. She couldn't help it. "Alike? *Us?*"

He just nodded calmly, completely unaffected by her scorn. "We're both opinionated. We're both driven. We both fight for our patients' well-being. We're both known for being stubborn." He stood.

"Oh, that's your brilliant analysis of the situation, is it?" Colleen asked, half-irritated, half-amused, as she slid out of the booth. "Well, you may be brilliant, but you're dead wrong."

"How's that?" Eric asked as he casually took her jacket from her hands. Colleen turned without thinking, letting him slip it on her. Only when she felt his knuckles graze her shoulder did her breath hitch in her lungs. She went completely still, her eyes widening, when she felt his hand slide beneath the trapped hair at her nape. He carefully withdrew the strands. His fingers furrowed through the tresses before he smoothed it next to her jacket.

Shivers ran down her spine.

He did *not* just do that, she told herself, her heart starting to hammer in her ears.

She had to put a stop to it or this thing with Eric was going to go from mutual dislike to sparking flirtation to epic catastrophe in record time.

She turned to face him, giving him an angelic smile.

"We are *not* similar at all. And I don't particularly like you."

She gave him a significant look and started to turn away, prepared to leave him standing in her proverbial dust. It'd serve him right for getting her all annoyed and agitated. He placed a hand on her shoulder, halting her. She glanced back. He leaned down until their faces were hardly six inches apart. This close, she caught his scent. The heady smell of subtle, spicy aftershave, clean skin and an elusive fragrance she could only identify as *man* filled her nose.

"That's where you make your mistake, Colleen," he said so quietly she was sure no one in the bustling restaurant could have heard him but her.

"What?" Colleen mumbled, set off balance by his sudden nearness.

"You *do* like me. You're just too stubborn to admit it," he said, his eyes glinting with humor, that infuriating smirk in place. He took her hand and started to lead her out of the restaurant. Colleen tugged, but he held fast. "Now, let's go pick out our invitations," he said, loud enough that Mrs. Pickens from the library and Pete Margaritte, who worked at the sawmill, both regarded them with avid interest as they passed. Colleen had no choice but to hurry after him, blushing profusely the whole time.

She'd agreed to be partners with him in this crime, after all. More fool her. She should have known from the beginning Eric Reyes would be way more than she'd bargained for.

"If you can just bring your invitation list for the engagement party to Brendan's room later today, I'll drop our combined list by Scrivener's this evening," Colleen told Eric twenty minutes later as they approached the hospital. Eric had led her to a back entrance in the administrative wing.

"We never got to discuss who we were going to invite in regard to our plan," Eric said as he held open the door for her.

"Plan?"

"Yeah, what we talked about yesterday," he said as they progressed down the silent corridor. "Operation Postpone Wedding, remember?"

"I knew what you meant. I was just hoping you'd reconsidered and given up on that idea."

His long-legged stride slowed in the empty hallway. "You don't think we should do it? You've decided Liam and Natalie aren't being impulsive?"

"No, I didn't say that. I think they should have a longer engagement. It's just..." She glanced over at him furtively. There was no way she could tell Eric that it had begun to annoy her that he was so utterly confident Liam and Natalie were behaving foolishly just because they were head over heels in love. Why should it matter to her that he was a romance cynic? She was usually so easygoing when it came to other people. Why did she have this overwhelming need to contradict everything Eric said?

"Never mind," Colleen said with a sigh, pausing in the empty hallway and facing him. "What were you planning?"

"Nothing major." He glanced to his right when a gray-haired man wearing a lab coat stepped out of one of the rooms. Eric and the other doctor greeted each other, and Eric turned to a door and opened it. Colleen realized belatedly they were in his office hallway.

"Come inside for a second, and I'll explain what I had in mind," he said, beckoning her into his office. He said it so casually, she was sure her sudden hesitance was pure paranoia. His manner had been nothing but agreeable and platonic ever since he'd pulled her out of Sultan's. He hadn't released her hand until they reached the street, and Colleen swore she could still feel the imprint of his fingers on her skin nearly half an hour later.

He removed his jacket and hung it on a coat tree near the door, the muscles beneath his shirt flexing in a distracting manner. Colleen blinked and trained her gaze on his profile.

"Well?" she prodded.

He took a step toward her, and Colleen resisted an urge to back away. Surely they weren't as close as it seemed. Eric just seemed to take up a lot of space in a room...or in her awareness, one of the two, she thought irritably.

"I was just going to put a few people on my list that might...highlight the relevant issue at the engagement party, that's all. And I thought *you* could put the other member of the unhappy couple on your list and—"

"Great. Our engagement party will look like an episode of the *Jerry Springer Show.*"

He laughed, the sound striking her as deep, rich and unrestrained. She crossed her arms beneath her breasts, instinctively defending herself. There was at least one woman in Harbor Town who wasn't going to turn to goo in the face of Eric's dark good looks and potent charm.

"It won't be that bad. I promise," he said, still grinning, his teeth appearing extra white next to his skin.

"Who did you have in mind to invite?" she asked curiously.

He mentioned two divorced couples they both knew. Her eyebrows arched in grudging respect at his choices.

"That just might work," Colleen had to concede. "Tony Tejada has been friends with Marc forever. Now he works closely with Liam at the Municipal Building. Tony went to bat for Liam, recommending him to the city council to fill the police chief position," she mused. Tony Tejada was Harbor Town's mayor, a friendly, well-liked man who, rumor had it, had spent more time and energy on his job than on his marriage.

"And I work on the surgical unit with Janice," Eric said, referring to Tony's ex-wife.

"I've been friends with Ellen Rappoport since we were in braces," Colleen continued, referring to half of the other couple Eric had mentioned. "Although I've never liked that husband of hers," she added pointedly.

"I'm not taking sides here. Cody and I are more acquaintances than friends. Natalie does Cody's taxes, and we occasionally trained for a marathon together two years ago."

"Well, he's a louse," Colleen stated, wanting to make her opinion clear. "He broke Ellen's heart with his womanizing, and that doesn't even take into account how Ellen's kids must be suffering. She took such a big chance in marrying him, and he swore he'd always be a father to her children, even though they were from her former marriage. He adopted them, for goodness' sake. I can't imagine how much Ellen and the kids must be hurting."

"Cody wasn't necessarily *womanizing*. He behaved stupidly with an old high-school sweetheart at a conference. Once."

"How can you defend him?"

Eric looked alarmed. "I'm not condoning his bad behavior. He was a fool, pure and simple. Even you have to admit, though, Cody represents our point pretty damn well."

She took an aggressive step toward him. "If you're implying my brother is even remotely like Cody Rappoport—"

"I'm *not*. I just meant that Cody and Ellen should have been a little more cautious about diving into marriage, especially with two innocent kids involved. I'm sure Ellen agrees with me, and likely Cody does, too."

She eyed him suspiciously, deciding he looked sufficiently contrite for his semidefense of a slimeball.

"All right," she mumbled. "All four of those people might

realistically be on our separate lists, even if we weren't attempting this silly plan."

"It's just a reality check," Eric reminded her, his voice low and compelling. She glanced up into his eyes and wished she hadn't. She couldn't seem to look away. "You know...to remind our siblings that passion can cloud the brain."

"Oh, yes. Because we all should be as rational and clear-headed as you," Colleen replied under her breath.

"What's that?" he asked, dipping his head toward her as though to hear her better.

"Nothing," she muttered, because much to her shock his face was now only inches away from hers, and those eyes she'd formerly designated as the bedroom variety were latched on to her mouth.

"Mind if I ask you a question?" She watched his firm, shapely lips moving as if in a trance.

"Okay," she murmured.

"Sixteen months ago I kissed you, and a few months later, you slugged me in the jaw in the parking lot at Jake's Place."

Her mouth fell open, but she didn't utter a word. She didn't know what shocked her more: the fact that Eric had brought up that kiss on Sunset Beach *again* or his reference to her impassioned, impulsive slug to his jaw last summer...or possibly the fact that said sexy jaw was now hovering mere inches away from her upturned face.

"I...I've never apologized for that. I'm really sorry," she whispered.

Just thinking about it mortified her. It'd been a hot, sultry night, and Eric had got into a confrontation with her brothers, Liam and Marc. Old emotions regarding the crash had boiled to the surface. Colleen had made a fool of herself by stopping the fight by jumping in front of her brothers and punching Eric herself.

Not one of her finer moments.

Eric and she were the only two people on the entire planet

who knew that impulsive act, in large part, related to what had occurred on Sunset Beach months before. That physical action was an admission, in a sense, that Eric had gotten to her, and he must know it. Colleen hadn't realized until that moment how much a secret tied you to another person. She struggled to think up an excuse for her volatile behavior that summer night.

"We Kavanaughs are rather…protective of one another. You know how family can be," she said apologetically.

"I do," he said in a hushed tone. "But I didn't bring it up because I was looking for an apology."

"No?"

He shook his head slowly. She couldn't pull her gaze off the firm, shapely lips centered above the indentation of that cleft on his chin. "I brought it up because I wanted to ask you something…something I've wondered about."

She stood frozen to the spot, even though she knew she should back away.

His dark head dipped slightly. His breath, warm and fragrant, brushed against her nose and lips. The subtle scent of his spicy aftershave filtered into her nose. She inhaled, greedy for it.

"Do you regret that kiss?" he asked.

For a stretched few seconds, neither spoke. The silence was absolute. Colleen wondered if they both held their breath.

"I keep *trying* to regret it but—"

She never finished her sentence, because he leaned down and closed the distance between them, seizing her mouth with his. One second she'd been Eric-less, and the next she was submerged in him, overwhelmed by the feeling of his demanding lips and singular taste. She stumbled in her boots. In fact, she later wondered with rising horror if she hadn't *swooned*. He caught her, holding her firmly in his arms.

But what woman *wouldn't* be caught off balance—and

thrilled by her dizziness—while being consumed by Eric Reyes?

She went up on her tiptoes and pressed against his long, lean body, her prickly nerve endings in need of pressure... sensation. It was if she'd been starving all this time and hadn't recognized her state of deprivation until now. He must have felt her desire, because he tightened his hands around her arms, pulling her closer still. His agile tongue demanded entry and she granted it, all too eager for his taste. He staked his claim, sweeping his tongue everywhere, exploring her. It thrilled her—his size, his strength. She wasn't used to feeling so small next to a man, so feminine in comparison.

One of his hands trailed up her arm, opened along the side of her neck in a thoroughly possessive gesture, devouring her all the while, making her hot...dizzy. The next thing she knew, his mouth was moving, awakening her nerve endings along her jaw and then her neck.

"You taste good enough to eat," he whispered roughly before he increased her shivers by placing a kiss on her ear. His ravishment of her throat continued. Colleen struggled to stand...to think.

In a remote part of her brain, she also recognized that he'd been restraining himself on Sunset Beach. Coming into contact with the full extent of his desire had her spinning.

"Eric...please...I don't think...such a good idea," she mumbled incoherently. Even as she attempted her lame protest, however, her actions told another story. Her hand found a way to his head. She held his mouth against her neck, delving her fingers into his thick, wavy hair.

He groaned when she scraped her fingernails against his scalp. He tightened his hold and pulled her higher and more firmly against him. Colleen gasped at the sensation of her breasts sliding along his chest. She twisted slightly against him, rubbing, needful of the friction his hard flesh offered her. He went still for a moment, his hot mouth at the base of her neck.

He lifted his hand from her shoulder, and Colleen heard the snick of the lock on the door.

Her eyes sprang open. The sound had been tiny, but full of meaning—charged, incendiary…illicit. She pushed against his chest and shoved out of his arms.

For a good five seconds, they stood there, both of them breathing heavily, several feet of space separating them. As the spell of his touch slowly faded, anger rushed in to take its place.

"What the hell do you think you're doing, locking that door?" she grated out.

He arched one brow sardonically, the expression telling her loud and clear that the answer was obvious.

She smoothed her shirt and took another step away from him. Not even her rising fury over what had just occurred could make her totally immune to the fact that Eric looked damn attractive at that moment. Her stroking fingers had mussed his hair. Several dark locks fell sexily onto his forehead.

And that wasn't all. His aroused state was shockingly—thrillingly—obvious, and he didn't appear to be in any haste to hide that fact from her.

The realization sent her into a tailspin. She was angry, true, but also bewildered by the strength of her response to him. She wanted Eric Reyes. *Eric Reyes*. She didn't *want* to want him, but her body seemed to be ignoring her wishes.

"I suppose this is some kind of ritual for you, to bring women to your office on your lunch hour," she said in a low, shaking voice. She reached to unfasten the lock.

"Always running, aren't you, Colleen? I always pegged you for having more courage than that."

Her hand dropped, and she spun to face him. "You ask me up to your office on a pretense and then take advantage of the situation and maul me. I choose to leave, and you claim that's running?" she said in a shaky voice.

He regarded her somberly. If it weren't for his mussed hair, smoky eyes and...*agitated* state, it might have been the return of the indomitable, arrogant Dr. Reyes. Seeing both aspects of his character in evidence—the cool, arrogant side alongside the hot, impassioned male—intrigued Colleen despite her irritation.

"If you want to leave, that's your prerogative, of course. I don't think it's me you're running from, though. Not me.... or my 'mauling' of your body," he added darkly.

Colleen flushed. He was right to chastise her for that mauling comment. If that had been mauling, then she was just as guilty for returning the favor.

"You're running because of the way you feel," he continued. "Why are you so determined to deny that we're attracted to each other?"

She rolled her eyes and released the lock. "The attraction would have to be a heck of a lot stronger than that for me to ever get involved with you," she said coldly, despite the fact that she was hot.

Very hot.

"Oh," he said, his head going back slightly as if he'd just caught her meaning. "A kiss has to be a lot better than that for the princess to be interested. I get it."

Her cheeks burned at his sarcasm. If his kiss had been any hotter, she might have spontaneously combusted. And he knew from experience how furious she became about that stupid "princess" reference.

"I'm not going to stand here and praise your sexual prowess, Reyes. I'm *not* interested. Now, do you want to play Dr. Don Juan, or do you want to plan this party and wedding with me?"

He dropped his arms and walked toward his desk. "I'm

definitely going to be in on the plans. This is my sister we're talking about."

"Fine," she said, her anger fizzling slightly at his refusal to fight with her. "Just…just keep your distance from me. This is family business only."

He paused behind his desk and met her stare across the room.

"I'll only get as close as what's required. I promise."

She nodded her head once in agreement and fled the room and was halfway down the hall before she realized the ambiguity of his solemn pledge.

Chapter Four

Mari Kavanaugh bustled into Colleen's kitchen, her high heels tapping briskly on the tile floor. The sounds of the band Eric had hired for the engagement party filtered through the swinging doors. Luckily, the event had fallen on a gorgeous fall evening. Colleen's terrace and family room had been transformed by a colorful silk pavilion, with lush autumn flower arrangements, glowing lanterns and flickering tea lights. Three giant heat lamps, donated by Eric, kept the terrace comfortable, and everyone seemed to be having a good time. Before she'd entered the kitchen a few minutes ago, Liam and Natalie had been the first to begin dancing.

Colleen had watched Liam and his fiancée dance, smiling wistfully just like every other guest at the party. The couple's love and desire for each other had been so evident it created an ache in Colleen's chest.

Her gaze had shifted when a tall figure moved into her line of sight. Colleen had watched a smiling Janice Tejada swaying in Eric Reyes's arms. Her sappy smile had evaporated.

She'd headed to the kitchen and began attacking a particularly grimy saucepan.

"We need more sweet-and-sour sauce," Mari said breathlessly as she flung open the refrigerator door. "The Asian dumplings are a big hit. I can't figure out how you're such a fabulous cook when your brother's idea of culinary preparation is dialing for takeout."

Her sister-in-law looked sophisticated and typically beautiful tonight, wearing a rust-colored dress and brown suede pumps. Colleen had been friends with Mari since they were in elementary school. They hadn't seen one another for fifteen years following the car crash, in which Mari's parents and Colleen's father had all been killed. Mari and Colleen had immediately connected again when Mari returned to Harbor Town, however. Colleen had been thrilled to see that Marc and Mari's passion for one another had burned brighter than ever. She *wasn't* a romantic, but it had seemed nothing but right in Mari and Marc's case when the star-crossed lovers finally got their happily ever after.

Mari kicked the refrigerator door shut and paused when she saw what Colleen was doing.

"Colleen, don't! Let the assistant Marc hired clean up. I can't believe you're doing dishes in that gorgeous dress," Mari scolded.

"Amanda is busy serving. Besides, I needed something to do."

Mari gave her a concerned glance. "Is everything all right? You seem preoccupied. All this party and wedding planning has been too much for you, hasn't it? Especially after all you did for Marc's and my wedding."

"I'm not too busy. I swear. I enjoy it," she insisted when she saw Mari's doubtful glance.

"I feel terrible. I'm Natalie's matron of honor, and Marc is Liam's best man, but you and Eric have been doing the lion's share of the work. It's not fair."

"It hasn't been difficult at all. Eric and I are here in town, and you're not. Mom has been helping out, as well. Here, stir it up before you serve it," Colleen directed, handing Mari a whisk for the sauce.

"I was surprised to hear Eric has been so involved in the planning," Mari said as she gave Colleen a sideways, speculative glance. "Hasn't that been…challenging for you?"

In truth, she *had* been spending too much time in Eric's presence lately. She'd been spending too much time *thinking* about Eric lately. Being forced into his company as they planned the upcoming nuptials had been both annoying and…stimulating.

"The two of you have always been like oil and water," Mari added.

"Or a lit fuse and dynamite?"

Mari chuckled. "I remember how worried I was about both of you working at The Family Center."

"I can't imagine why. Did it have anything to do with the fact that I slugged him in the parking lot of Jake's Place a few days before you hired me?" Colleen muttered wryly.

Mari paused and leaned her hip against the counter, a curious expression on her face. "You know, I always wondered about that. I've never known you to act that way. I mean, emotions were certainly running high that night. But while you've always had a temper, I've never known you to get physical. Why *does* Eric bother you so much?"

Colleen scrubbed at the pan extra hard. It was a good question, and she wasn't sure how much she should reveal. Mari didn't know that she and Eric had kissed on Sunset Beach just weeks before she'd punched him in a whirlwind of fury and bewilderment.

"He's insufferable," she said.

Mari laughed and picked up the ladle. "You're the only person on the planet who thinks so. Most women adore him. He's smart, he's handsome, he's charming, he's great with kids. If I recall correctly," Mari said, giving Colleen a sly glance, "you were right there like the rest of us when we were teenagers, waiting for Eric to take off his shirt while he worked for that landscaping company. You did your fair share of drooling whenever he did, too."

Colleen snorted with laughter. Their mirth was interrupted by the sound of the music getting louder and the squeak of the swinging door. Both women glanced around, but Mari recovered at the sight of Eric faster than Colleen.

"Hey." Mari greeted him with a grin. "We were just talking about you. You and Colleen should be proud. The party is a huge success."

Colleen's wide grin faded as her gaze ran down Eric's body. He looked beyond good, wearing a dark blue suit that set off the width of his shoulders and trim hips. His dress shirt seemed appealingly white next to his bronzed skin. His hair looked almost black against the contrast of his collar.

When he'd come over earlier to help prepare for the party, her heart had seemed to jerk in her chest. Had he always been so handsome? She'd known he was good-looking, of course. Most women in Harbor Town knew that. But the intensity of his attractiveness, his sheer sexual potency, seemed to have escaped her until now.

Or it had until that kiss last summer.

"Liam and Natalie *were* having a terrific time," Eric said.

Colleen set down the dish towel and smoothed her dress over her hips, trying to ignore the fact that Eric's gaze flickered downward, following the path of her hands. "What do you mean?" she asked, concerned.

"It's Tony Tejada and Janice," he told her. For the first time, she realized his jaw looked tense. "Tony didn't take to me dancing with Janice very well."

"Eric, you didn't—" Colleen began in a rush, suspicious that he'd "tweaked" events a little too stringently in order to make his precious point about the foolishness of impulsive romance and marriage.

"Oh, no—" Mari muttered at the same time Colleen spoke, but both of them were cut off as Tony stormed into the kitchen. He was about a head and a half shorter than Eric, but he had the muscular build of a one-time athlete. Eric met his angry gaze levelly.

"I would prefer it if you kept your hands off my wife," Tony said aggressively.

"Your *ex-wife* is my friend and coworker. And we were just dancing. If you don't want to see Janice in someone else's arms, I suggest you ask her to dance yourself." Given Tony's agitation, Colleen couldn't help but respect Eric's cool, even response. Eric turned his dark-eyed gaze to her.

"Actually, I came looking for you," he told Colleen before Tony could utter another word.

"Uh…you did?" Colleen noticed Tony's neck had turned brick-red above his collar as he glared at Eric.

"Yes." He held out a hand toward her. "Come and dance with me."

Colleen wavered, confused by the turn of events. Tony looked furiously flummoxed, Mari appeared amused and Eric just stood there, his face completely impassive, his arm stretched toward her in a beckoning gesture.

"Er…okay," she muttered gracelessly. Dancing with Eric would separate him and Tony, which Colleen thought was a pretty darn good idea at the moment. When she placed her hand in his, he immediately swept her into his arms. He moved her gracefully out of the kitchen and beyond the patio and the pavilion until they were beneath the star-spangled, ebony dome of the night sky. The brisk autumn air felt nice against her heated skin.

Natalie and Liam and several other couples were also swaying to the jazz music, but they remained beneath the silk pavilion, closer to the patio doors. Colleen fleetingly noticed Natalie's pinched expression of concern as she glanced at her brother. Had Natalie noticed Tony Tejada's anger?

"Is it your mission in life to make trouble wherever you go?" Colleen hissed. Eric hadn't touched her since that kiss in his office nine days ago. He'd been nothing but polite and businesslike as they planned the engagement party together. She'd convinced herself she was glad he hadn't tried to touch her again...or kiss her...

She'd hadn't entirely convinced herself, apparently. The heat and pressure of his hand resting on her hip was making her breathless.

He leaned back slightly and looked into her face. "A dance is trouble?"

"Not *this* dance," Colleen grated out, trying to ignore the sensation of his flat belly, pelvis and thighs brushing against her own. "I'm talking about the fact that you were flirting with Janice while you danced. You *knew* Tony was watching. You were putting your little plan into place...plotting. I thought you said you weren't going to do anything malicious to make your point," she said accusingly and with the deepest of sarcasm.

His dark brows rose. "I wasn't plotting. That happened all of its own accord. And I wasn't *flirting*."

Colleen made a disgusted noise. "I was watching. You were so flirting."

"You were?" Eric asked, his question confusing her. He moved the hand on her hip to the middle of her back and pushed her slightly toward him. The contact between their bodies increased. Her breasts brushed against the lapel of his suit jacket, making her breath catch in her throat.

Colleen glanced up instinctively into his face. In her heels, her eye level was just above his mouth.

"I...I was...*what?*"

"Watching me?" he clarified while she studied his lips

moving. When she realized what she was doing, her gaze zipped up to meet his.

"Not everyone is watching you," she said, exasperated.

He chuckled. "I wasn't asking about everyone," he replied, smiling in the face of her sarcasm.

As usual.

Before she could give him a blistering response, the music swelled and he spun and dipped her expertly. She laughed in surprised delight when he spun her again. She was suddenly back swaying in his arms, neither of them missing a beat.

"Where did an ex-hockey player learn moves like that?" she asked, still grinning.

"Dancing with the Stars?" he asked.

She gave him a *give me a break* look, and he chuckled.

"I had a girlfriend in college who loved dancing. We took a few lessons together."

"Hmm... Well, I suppose it makes sense that you're a good dancer. Natalie's brilliant. You two must have gotten good genes. So, what happened to the girlfriend?"

He looked puzzled.

"The dancing one," Colleen clarified.

"Oh." He shrugged, the movement of his jacket sliding against her body causing her breasts to tingle. Had he just pulled her subtly closer?

"It was college. Time to experiment a little. Didn't you date a lot in college?"

"No. I started dating Darin my sophomore year."

"And you were only with him until you were married?"

"Yes," Colleen replied a little sharply. In truth, Darin had been the *only* man she'd ever been with. "What's wrong with that? Are you so anti romance that you don't believe young people can fall in love and remain faithful to one another?"

"I'm at a loss as to when I've given you the impression I'm anti romance. I can assure you, I'm very much on the pro side."

She just stared for a second, her mouth slightly open. His voice had gone husky. She blinked and willed herself to look into her backyard.

"You mean that you're on the pro side in regard to sex. I'd hardly call that romance," she said coolly.

"Really? That's a shame."

She gave him a withering glance, which bounced right off him.

"I don't consider sex to be a casual matter in the slightest," he murmured.

"I can imagine if I did a survey of the women you've dated recently, they might disagree."

Colleen's eyes widened when he lowered his chin and brushed it against her temple. His breath felt warm near her ear. "I doubt any one of those women would tell you I was anything but completely serious and focused when it comes to that particular topic."

"Well, *I* would have to be interested in order to ask one of them. Which I'm not."

"No?"

"Not even close," she assured him.

"Are you implying that you're not interested in the topic in general?" he asked without missing a beat, leaning back to study her face. "Or just in regard to me?"

Colleen laughed. She couldn't help it. He looked completely earnest, like he was asking a professor for clarification on a puzzling math problem.

"I'm just not interested," she told him, not unkindly. When she noticed his quizzical look, she added, "It's got nothing to do with you personally."

"Of course not."

"I'm serious."

For a few seconds, they regarded each other somberly while they moved together to the music. Colleen felt an increasingly familiar feeling of wanting to move closer to him.

Her misguided attraction must have outweighed wisdom somewhat, because she did indeed find herself moving a hairsbreadth closer. When she registered the smoky look that entered his eyes, she knew he'd noticed.

"You're holding back," he pronounced suddenly, as if he'd taken a moment to scan her mind with that brilliant brain of his and had just come to a conclusion. "You are cynical about romance, true…but it's more than that. You *do* object specifically to me. What is it you don't like about me?"

Colleen swallowed and glanced blindly at the other couples circling beneath the pumpkin-colored canopy, lanterns glowing around their moving feet. Two weeks ago, she would have had no problem whatsoever giving Eric Reyes a list of reasons why she didn't like him. *Arrogant, stubborn, know-it-all* might have topped the list.

But things had changed in the past ten days. After seeing his stellar, compassionate treatment of Brendan, both in the hospital and post-discharge, in addition to spending time with him planning the engagement party, Colleen recognized that while Eric was opinionated, he was by no means unreasonable. He was intelligent and a good listener, too.

He tilted one eyebrow up at her when she didn't speak, and Colleen found herself growing desperate for something reasonable to say. She certainly couldn't tell him she didn't like him because he set her off balance. Colleen was confident, given the parameters of her known world. Eric made her second-guess herself. He made her self-conscious and irritable and…worked up.

"I told you," she said firmly. "It's got nothing to do with you. I haven't dated that much. Not since Darin died."

He was quiet for a moment. "You're young, Colleen. Not to mention extremely beautiful. Do you really plan to stay celibate forever?" She blinked and met his stare, set off guard by his solemn tone when he'd called her beautiful. One glance into those compelling eyes and she knew it hadn't been casual flattery.

"That's none of your concern," she said quietly.

"I beg to differ. I'm very concerned about it."

The music came to an end. Her heart drumming in her ears, Colleen turned and walked toward the patio doors without glancing back. Her skin tingled, as if in protest over the sudden loss of the heat and the pressure of his body.

I'm very concerned about it.

The thought of him murmuring those words caused a slight shudder to go through her. She willed herself to resume the role of hostess, smiling and chatting with guests, forcing the unsettling recollection out of her mind. The back of her neck prickled and she glanced around, only to see Eric's eyes were on her as he, too, socialized. He smiled as he spoke—a small, secret smile. Too late, she realized she was returning the smile across her crowded family room and had completely lost track of her conversation.

"I know, I thought it was funny, too," Gail Sossinot said, interrupting her husband Emmett's story about a ladder that had folded up while he'd been on it doing repairs. Colleen had asked her guest about the bandage he'd been wearing on his wrist. Her cheeks turned warm.

"I'm sorry," she said contritely. "A sprained wrist isn't funny. I was…thinking of something else." Colleen fumbled to apologize for her faux pas. She'd been caught engaging in some unintentional nonverbal flirtation.

It annoyed her that no matter whom she spoke to, or what the topic of conversation was, she was aware of Eric's every move, as if he possessed some kind of magnetic pull. She doubted anyone would have guessed she was anything but a calm, engaged hostess, but Colleen knew the truth.

Her brain and body were buzzing. She was stirred up after that dance, and it was all Eric's fault.

An hour or so later, she noticed the party was thinning

out. She was satisfied with their efforts. With the exception of Tony Tejada's bout of jealousy in regard to his ex-wife, everyone seemed to have had a great time, most importantly Natalie and Liam. Perhaps her censorious speech toward Eric while they danced had been effective, because he hadn't tried to stir the pot in regard to the other acrimonious couple they'd invited to the party. Her friend Ellen Rappoport had settled for shooting venomous stares at her ex-husband from across the crowded room while her ex, Cody, looked contrite and uncomfortable, and made an early exit. Although Natalie had sadly commented to Colleen about the tension between Cody and Ellen, she hadn't seemed to take the couple's unhappiness to heart personally.

Colleen spoke with her brother Marc and her mother, took a few drink orders from the remaining guests, and headed to the kitchen.

She walked into a scene of confusion.

Mari and Natalie glanced up at the sound of her entrance. Both looked concerned. For some reason, her brother Liam was crouched on the floor next to someone who sat in one of Colleen's kitchen chairs—Janice Tejada. She was crying energetically.

"How dare he? Tony never had the time for me and the kids when we were married, but now that the divorce is final, he has the nerve to make a scene at a party because he's jealous?" Janice exclaimed wetly to Liam. She took one of the tissues Liam offered her and blew her nose. "I'm sorry," she wailed. "I know I shouldn't be going on like this at your engagement party—"

"Hey, don't worry about that," Liam consoled, and Natalie seconded his words. "What are friends for, if not to support each other during times like this?"

Liam glanced up at Colleen in alarm when, instead of being soothed by their consolations, Janice sobbed even harder. Colleen bustled over to the fridge and took out a can of ginger ale. She poured some of the bubbly liquid into a glass and brought it over to Janice.

"Here, drink this, Janice," Colleen soothed. Liam looked relieved when Janice sniffed and hiccupped and took the proffered glass. He stood and moved back, seeming glad to cede his role as comforter to his sister. Colleen took his place, pulling up a chair.

She took Janice's hand in both of her own and patted it while Janice drank her ginger ale. Janice's crying slowly ebbed, and she looked up at Colleen, misery evident in every aspect of her expression.

"I'll never understand men," Janice sniffed.

Colleen nodded in agreement. "You think you have them figured out, and then you realize that was just the first layer of wrapping paper."

Janice gave a pressured laugh and mopped at her wet cheeks with wads of tissue. Colleen was only vaguely aware of the kitchen door swinging open. It was in her nature to focus her entire attention on someone who was in distress... to help that person through their storm. She supposed that instinct was what had first prodded her to become a counselor.

"I thought we were supposed to be the uncomplicated ones," Liam murmured humorously from behind them.

"You are...during the first ecstatic throes of infatuation," Colleen mused without taking her eyes off Janice. "It doesn't take an Einstein to figure out what men want then."

Janice gave a teary snort. "Exactly. But after a few years of marriage, and children, and night feedings, and busy schedules and hard choices and conflict...well, like Colleen said. Men turn just as convoluted and bewildering as women."

"More so, because at least we admit we're confused. Men insist on clinging to the myth that they're one hundred percent rational all the time," Mari said from behind her.

"But how can Tony rationalize acting like a caveman when

he sees me dancing with another man? He gave up his right to me when he agreed to the divorce, didn't he?" Janice's gaze was imploring, as if she were begging Colleen to back up her claim.

Colleen rubbed Janice's hand soothingly. "A signature on a piece of paper can't truly eliminate all the feelings Tony must have for you. It's not that simple, Janice."

Janice lowered her tissue-clutching hand slowly. "You... you think Tony still cares about me?" she asked in a quavering voice.

Colleen hesitated. Surely the logical thing to do was to provide some cliché in regard to Janice getting on with her life and time healing all wounds.

And yet...

"Of course he still cares about you," Colleen said softly. "Don't you notice the way he watches your every move from across a crowded room?"

"It's true," Liam said from behind her. "Tony has always been crazy about you, Janice. He's never spoken his feelings out loud to me in regard to the divorce, but I can see regret written on every line of his face. Regret and guilt. I know he feels responsible for things going south in the marriage. I see him almost every day at the Municipal Building, and he hasn't been the same since you two split."

"He's never *told* me that," Janice said in a whispery, tentative voice.

"Since when can a man ever talk about his feelings?" Colleen said, patting Janice's hand. "Sometimes actions speak louder than words. I can't speak for Tony, of course, but would he really have gotten so jealous tonight when he saw you dancing with Eric if he didn't still have feelings? If I were you, I'd go and talk to him," she urged earnestly. "Right now. Quickly. Before both of you have time to put bandages on your feelings and retreat into your respective corners. Maybe there's still a chance to resolve things. Who knows?"

Janice set down her ginger ale and gave her cheeks one last swipe. "Do you really think so?"

"Absolutely," Liam and Natalie said in unison.

Colleen stood along with Janice. "He still cares about you, Janice," she said. "I suspect you still care a lot about him. Talking honestly is the right thing to do, no matter what the end result is."

Janice sniffed and gave Colleen a quick hug. She gave Mari, Liam and Natalie a thankful glance before she hurried out of the room, obviously intent on following Colleen's recommendation.

Colleen turned her head at the sound of someone clearing his throat.

Her eyes widened at the sight of Eric leaning against the counter, his arms crossed beneath his chest, his eyes smoldering. He'd been watching the whole exchange—and her—with apparent interest. His lips tilted into a small, sardonic grin.

Embarrassment flooded her.

She'd just been caught in the act. Of all the people at this party, why had Eric Reyes had to be a witness to her bout of romantic advice-giving?

Chapter Five

She broke eye contact with Eric.

"This kitchen is getting too crowded," she said after Janice had left the room. She pointed at Eric. "You, take out a fresh bowl of dip, please, and you—" she transferred her finger to her brother "—go and dance with your fiancée and have a terrific time."

"Don't even try and argue with her," Liam told Eric from the side of his mouth as he passed him, Natalie's hand in his. "I grew up with her. We called her the little general. Resistance is futile."

Colleen smiled and rolled her eyes at Liam's joke, but she still had difficulty meeting Eric's gaze. She noticed that he'd opened the refrigerator door and was following her instructions. To her horror, Mari excused herself to get some bottles of soda from the garage, and she was left alone with Eric in the kitchen. She bustled over to the cabinet and pretended to be utterly involved with the fascinating task of setting glasses on the counter.

Damn it, she thought irritably as she gave him a sideways glance. How did he do smug so effortlessly?

"So, what was that all about?" he murmured, leaning against the counter. With that infamous little smirk, lazy pose and immaculate suit, he looked ready for the glossy page of a men's magazine.

"What?" she replied airily.

"That. What just happened with Janice," he said, nodding toward the table.

She glanced away, her expression stubborn. "A guest was upset. I consoled her."

"Whatever happened to demonstrating the dangers of a quick marriage for Liam and Natalie's sake? You sounded more like an advice columnist for *True Romance Confidential* than someone demonstrating the value of wisdom and logic when it comes to love."

Her irritation went on instant froth-mode.

"True Romance Confidential," she snorted. "You just made that up. There was nothing wrong with the advice I gave Janice," she said defensively when he gave her a bland look.

"So...you weren't being completely honest when you said you agreed with me that two people shouldn't be so impulsive when it came to love," he said in a mellow tone, completely ignoring her rising fury. "I'm starting to think you're a closet romantic, Colleen."

"Well, here's what *I* think about what *you* think, Reyes—" she burst out heatedly, then paused when she heard Mari's quick footsteps in the back hallway.

"I'd better go and replace the dip," he said, smiling.

"Yeah. You'd better." She flung open the freezer door and reached for the ice.

"Is everything okay, Colleen?" Mari asked a few seconds later, probably noticing the loud clanking noise Colleen made as she tossed ice cubes into glasses with undue force.

"Of course. I'm fine," she mumbled, taking a deep breath and exhaling. Why did she let him get to her? Who cared what Eric thought about her? "But I should know better than to get involved in Janice and Tony's family conflict."

"I disagree. I'm glad you said what you did to Janice. Marc thinks it was a real shame those two ever broke up. Janice and Tony were the perfect example of a communication breakdown. They never really did talk in all the months leading up to their divorce," Mari said as she placed a tray on the counter and arranged the glasses on it. She gave Colleen a significant glance. "Besides, I think we both know it's best to be open about this stuff. Pushing things down never helped in the long run. Secrets are toxic."

"That's the truth," Colleen admitted, thinking about past Kavanaugh family secrets. Silence hadn't done much to alleviate the pain of those secrets once they were revealed. In fact, the years of silence had made the truth even more painful when it was finally brought to the surface.

"Which reminds me...have you heard from Deidre?" Mari asked as Colleen poured cranberry juice into one of the glasses. She glanced up, noticing the tension in Mari's tone. Her sister-in-law's thoughts had obviously taken the same path as her own.

Deidre Kavanaugh was Colleen's sister. During the summer, they'd all learned that Derry Kavanaugh wasn't Deidre's biological father. Deidre had been conceived during an extramarital affair Brigit had had with billionaire business mogul, Lincoln DuBois. Liam had gone to Germany, where Deidre had been working as a nurse in order to break the devastating news. He'd brought her back to the States, and now Deidre was at Lincoln DuBois's Lake Tahoe mansion.

"Just yesterday," Colleen replied in a hushed voice. "Her..." She paused, unable to say the word *father*. She still hadn't gotten used to the fact that Deidre's biological father wasn't Derry Kavanaugh, but Lincoln DuBois. "DuBois isn't doing very well at all. They had thought that he'd lost so much of his functioning because of several strokes, but recently Deidre insisted he be taken to the hospital for extensive brain imaging. Sure enough, they found a tumor in an area where they can't operate. Deidre sounds fairly certain that he doesn't have very long to live."

Mari made a sound of distress. "I can't imagine what she must be going through, out in Lake Tahoe, all alone...tending to a dying man...a man she just learned was her father months ago."

"I know," Colleen said grimly. "I'm glad that Liam and Marc have both visited her. I keep offering as well, but she insists she'd rather wait for me to come when...you know..." She trailed off, knowing Mari would understand she referred to the inevitable approaching death of Lincoln DuBois.

"She'll need you at her side the most then," Mari said, taking an empty club-soda bottle from Colleen and throwing it in the recycle bin. She glanced at Colleen sadly. "And Deidre still refuses to speak to Brigit?"

She nodded. "She's adamant about not seeing Mom. You know Deidre. She's a force of nature when she makes up her mind about something. She blames Mom for everything. I try to talk to her about starting slowly with reconciliation—testing the waters—but Deidre is so hurt, you know? She's even refusing to attend the wedding, because she doesn't want to see Mom."

Mari opened her mouth to reply, compassion in her eyes, but was interrupted by the kitchen door swinging open and the sound of energetic Latin music filtering into the kitchen.

"The natives are getting restless for those drinks after some impromptu rumbaing," Marc Kavanaugh told his wife, an amused look on his handsome face. Mari snorted and grabbed the drink tray.

"I'm sorry I missed you doing the rumba," she told her

husband as she walked toward the door. "I hope you didn't throw a hip out or anything."

"My hips are in perfect working order," Marc murmured, stroking his wife's lower back. "I keep them well-tuned, in deference to you."

"They're well-tuned *because* of me," Mari replied very softly, laughter in her voice. They kissed briefly and walked out of the kitchen.

Colleen wasn't supposed to overhear their teasing, intimate little exchange, but she had. She also didn't miss Marc's special grin meant just for his wife or the way he caressed Mari's hip in such an appreciative manner.

A strange feeling went through her. Was it envy? Longing for the kind of relationship Marc and Mari had?

All this wedding planning is making you miss Darin, that's all, she told herself as she screwed the cap on a soda bottle.

Deep down, she knew that mental reassurance wasn't entirely correct. Darin's death had left an empty hole in her life, but this current feeling of longing, while not wholly unfamiliar, was not something she associated to her late husband. Darin and she had been the best of friends, entirely comfortable with one another. Their sex life had been good. They'd both been young and healthy and eager to express their love for each other physically.

But still, what she'd experienced with Darin had felt…controllable. There was no sense of tumbling dangerously head over heels or potentially sacrificing too much. She knew he would leave her while he was on duty for extended periods of time. She knew how dangerous his work was as an Army Ranger. She'd mentally prepared herself for periods apart from him, although who could totally prepare themselves for that final, most difficult separation?

Darin's death had been hard— beyond hard—but she'd endured.

She hated to admit it to herself, but since his death, part

of her had been glad she hadn't been in that wild, fevered, impassioned kind of love with Darin. How could she have survived after his death if she'd surrendered every last shred of herself?

Following her father's death, Colleen had been desperate for stability and certainty. The known world of her family life had suddenly crumbled. Her once respected and adored father was dead, maligned by the press and townspeople. Her sister, Deidre, left Harbor Town, never to return.

When she'd met Darin at nineteen, she'd immediately been attracted to his easy charm, amiable personality, and desire and ability to care for her unconditionally. She'd loved Darin. Part of her always would. But they hadn't shared the deep, passionate connection she observed between Marc and Mari or Liam and Natalie.

But you'd thought your parents shared that same respect and passion, the niggling voice in her head said. *Look what was hiding in the dusty, dark corners of that seemingly ideal relationship: infidelity, lies, secrets...*

She slammed the cupboard door closed with a bang, willing the troublemaking voice in her head to shut up.

Around midnight Colleen said her goodbyes to the last guests and shut the front door. Eric, Mari and Marc insisted they wanted to help her clean up, but she protested, shooing them out the door. She'd prefer to attack things in the morning. Colleen couldn't keep her mother from staying, though. Fortunately, the babysitter watching Brendan, Jenny, and Marc and Mari's daughter, Riley, at her mother's house had been hired to stay overnight and well into the morning. Together they made a good dent in the cleanup.

When Brigit finally left at close to 1:00 a.m., Colleen breathed a sigh of relief. She rubbed her neck as she walked down the dim hallway, feeling exhausted but happy. The party had been a success. It'd been a long day, and it was late. The thought of getting out of her heels and diving into bed was enticing.

She started and paused when she heard a tap on the front door. She hurried back and flipped on the front porch light.

"Did you forget something," she asked as she opened the door, halting when she saw it wasn't her mother, but Eric. He'd changed out of his suit. He stood on her small front porch, hands in his front pockets. He looked just as appealing in jeans, T-shirt and a casual jacket than he had in his well-cut, expensive suit. She shoved the thought aside.

"What are you doing here?" she asked, stunned.

"I started to feel bad about leaving when there was still stuff to be done."

"Don't be silly," she admonished. "Everything is all cleaned up. There's nothing left to do but go to bed."

The silence seemed to swell and press on her eardrums in the seconds that followed. Colleen mentally replayed what she'd just said and blushed.

"I really didn't come over to help you clean up," he suddenly said.

She crossed her arms under her breasts, trepidation causing her backbone to straighten. "You didn't?"

He shook his head, holding her stare. "I wanted to talk to you about something. Do you mind?" he asked, nodding toward her family room.

She sighed and opened the door all the way. She minded all right, but not because she was tired. Her fatigue had melted out of her during some point while Eric and she regarded each other silently, only to be replaced by a nervous sort of anticipation. He followed her down the hallway into her family room. She paused in front of the fireplace and turned to face him. "What is it?" she asked.

He nodded toward the couch. "Why don't you sit down? You must be tired. You were on the move all night, and those heels don't look very foot friendly." She shifted self-consciously when she noticed his appreciative glance at her stiletto-clad feet.

"I'm fine standing," she said, even though her feet ached like crazy. "What did you need to talk to me about?" she asked, not at all sure she wanted to hear his answer.

Eric studied her before he answered. Colleen was always beautiful, but tonight she looked sinful in an emerald-green dress and a pair of sexy, strappy black leather heels. He hadn't been able to keep his eyes off her legs all night. Or the bounce of her lush, golden hair…or her pink lips…or the way the clinging fabric of her dress emphasized the shape of her breasts, her hips, her…

He cleared his throat and took a step toward her, resting one of his hands on the mantel.

"I'm getting the impression our plan isn't going to work," he said.

"You're not going to start lecturing me about Janice Tejada, are you? I'm not going to apologize for what I said to her. I'm a therapist. I have to rely on instinct, and my instinct told me at that moment I should say what I said."

He raised one eyebrow. "But your instinct also tells you Liam and Natalie are rushing into things," he pointed out.

"Your scheme isn't going to work. Not because I disagree about Natalie and Liam being rash, but because—"

"It's none of our business," Eric finished for her, already having come to the same conclusion.

"Exactly."

"Well, you can't blame a big brother for trying," he mused. His gaze skittered across a framed photo of a man with dark gold, close-clipped hair in military uniform.

"Darin?" he asked.

"Yes."

"You miss him a lot, don't you?"

"Did you come over here to ask me about Darin?" she asked, a trifle impatiently.

"Maybe," he admitted.

She gave him an exasperated glance, and he grinned. He'd grown accustomed to her irritation with him over the past week and a half. Maybe he'd grown used to it because her bouts of annoyance seemed increasingly just for show, and they both knew it. His attraction for her grew every second he spent with her. Colleen was like a drug. The more she let down her guard and showed him her vibrant spirit, the more he wanted to drown in it.

The truth was, they were getting used to each other. The truth was, Colleen liked him. It was time for him to push her, just a tad, into admitting that fact.

"Is Darin the reason you refuse to go out with me?"

Her expression flattened. Her clear, bluish-green eyes went huge in her face. Apparently he'd taken her by surprise.

Good.

"I wasn't aware of the fact that you'd ever asked me out," she blurted.

He glanced up at the ceiling, pretending to consider. "You're right. Maybe I haven't ever officially. I would have thought my intentions were clear, though."

She made an incredulous sound.

"No?" he asked.

"If you're talking about your insinuation that you wanted to sleep with me while we were dancing tonight, then you definitely were *not* clear. Wanting to go to bed with someone and asking them on a date are two completely different things." She pushed a tendril of hair behind her shoulder in a nervous gesture. He noticed the rapid throb of her pulse at her throat. He wanted to touch her. Whether to soothe her or excite her, he didn't know, but the desire to feel his skin against hers felt so powerful it was like a stab of pain.

"Okay. If you say so. Will you go out on a date with me, then?" he asked quietly.

Her eyes flashed. "No."

"Then that takes me back to my original question. Is it because you're still mourning your late husband?"

"No."

"Then I *was* right earlier—it *is* about me. Haven't I proven to you at this point that I'm not the SOB you were always making me out to be?"

"Eric," she began in a pressured manner and then halted. "I don't think you're an SOB."

"You used to. You never made a secret of that."

Color stained her cheeks. He glanced down and saw that the small triangle of skin exposed at her chest had deepened in color, as well. Her breasts rose in agitation. He dragged his gaze back up to her face with an effort.

"I know it. And I'm sorry. I haven't really thought that for a while now. You're...you're okay."

"High praise indeed, coming from you. Was that a proposal?"

"Ha," she scoffed. Still, her defenses were wavering. She looked more uncertain than annoyed. Vulnerability made her even more beautiful, impossible though that seemed. "My point is, I like you fine. You're nowhere near as arrogant as I thought you were. That doesn't mean I want to..." She paused. Eric watched through a narrowed gaze as she bit at her lower lip. His body responded like she'd just reached out and stroked him where it counted. He moved a few inches closer to her, his actions directed by pure instinct.

"...go out with you," she finished in a tremulous voice.

"I promise I'll be patient, Colleen. I'll go slow, if that's what you want. I'll go fast, if that's what you prefer. Whatever you want. Just know that I'll take very, very good care of you," he murmured, dropping his head nearer to hers. She didn't move away, just looked up at him with a big-eyed stare that made him feel one part tender and one part like the big bad wolf.

"Will you please stop looking at me like that?" she whispered.

"I can't seem to help it. Can't seem to stop this, either," he admitted before he cradled the side her neck in his hand and kissed her. She made a sound in her throat like a desperate whimper and returned the kiss.

He'd kept himself on a tight leash ever since that day in his office, but his restraint tank was now officially on empty. Spending time with her this past week, seeing the way her eyes lit up when she laughed, watching her move gracefully amongst the guests all evening, holding her in his arms while they danced—all of it had worn him thin. A man could only take so much, no matter how rational that man was.

Besides, all it took was touching Colleen once, and he became the polar opposite of rational. Losing himself in pure feeling had never felt so good.

He reacquainted himself with the shape of her mouth, gloried in how responsive she was, how soft. The heat just behind her lips beckoned him. He stroked her with his tongue, and she opened for him. He groaned and put his hands on her hips, pulling her against him. The feeling of her curving flesh covered by clinging knit fabric made everything go red for a moment. He leaned over her, trying to slake himself on her taste. The more he drank of her, the more he touched, the more he wanted. His hands moved hungrily, detailing her back, the ridge of her spine.

He molded her hips in his palms before he traced the curve that led to her narrow waist. So soft. So feminine. Her rib cage felt narrow and delicate in his cradling palms. He could feel her heart beating rapidly inside of it. When he touched the side of her breast and felt firm, luscious flesh, they each moaned into the other's mouth.

He lifted his head and studied her face as he shaped her

breast to his palm. A shudder of excitement went through her. Her eyelids opened a crack. Her eyes looked glassy, her lips pink and slightly puffy from his ravening kiss.

"You're so beautiful," he muttered through a tight jaw. "Have I told you that?"

"Yes," she mumbled. "While we danced."

"It wasn't enough. I want to tell you more. I want to show you."

His thumb found her nipple, and he stroked her. He stayed immobile, but it was as if his entire body leapt in arousal. Even through her bra, he felt how she stiffened in response to his caress. He cradled the weight of her breast and molded her flesh against his hand, teasing the nipple into further pronouncement with his thumb and forefinger.

She closed her eyes and gasped, arching her spine slightly and pressing their hips together tightly. He winced in pleasure at the sensation. Unable to resist the lure of her parted lips, he plucked at her mouth, consuming her...coaxing her.

His hand traveled down the length of her body, exploring her hip and the taut, delicious curve of a buttock. He'd wanted to touch her so much over the past several days. Being able to do so now—feeling her firm, feminine flesh, hearing her little moans of excitement—felt like the height of sensual gratification.

Having her touch him was just as intoxicating. Her hands caressed his lower back, and then his hips. She stroked his outer thigh as though she was trying to feel the shape of the muscle through his clothing. Her enthusiastic caresses drove him a little nuts. If their bodies pressed any closer, he was going to be inside—

She bit at him gently, dragging his lower lip between her front teeth. A shudder of pleasure went through him. His eyes sprang wide.

Enough already.

He sealed their torrid kiss with a low growl of arousal. His hands on her waist, he urged her to follow him. She gave a little shriek of surprise when he fell back on her couch, bringing her with him until she partially sprawled on top of him. He shifted his hands beneath the fabric of her dress, relishing the sensation of long, silk-clad legs. He grabbed just above her knees and pulled, sliding her along his legs and firmly into his lap. His jaw clamped tight at the sensation of her breasts crushed against his chest, their bellies pressed tight... the heat from their arousal mingling.

Her lips were still parted in surprise at their sudden transfer of position. He laced his fingers through her long hair and cradled her head, kissing her hard before she had a chance to speak. His other hand opened along the length of a silky thigh. She shifted subtly in his lap as she kissed him, making it harder and harder for him to control himself.

One hand trailed up her back and found the tab of her dress zipper. The sound of it lowering was like a hiss of arousal. Her skin was warm and satin-soft between the parting fabric. He poked his hand beneath the dress and spread his hand over the back of her ribs, greedy to absorb the sensation of her.

He groaned and broke their heated kiss. How was it that a small patch of skin on a woman's back could make him so desperate?

"I'm taking you to bed," he proclaimed gruffly.

"What?" she mumbled.

He paused in the action of preparing to shift her in his lap so he could lift her in his arms. He *shouldn't* have paused, but he did. She hadn't sounded uncertain, necessarily, just dazed.

"To bed," he repeated. He gave a small smile when he saw how befuddled she looked...how gorgeous. Unable to refrain, he nipped at her bee-stung lower lip. "You do have one of those, don't you?"

"Of course I do," she mouthed, even though no sound

came out of her mouth as she stared at his face as if she'd never seen him before.

"Mari told me earlier the kids were at your mother's. We're all alone, Colleen. It's just you and me."

Her beautiful, desire-glazed eyes went wide.

Abruptly, she pushed herself out of his arms. She stood clumsily. One moment, he held a sex-softened, eager female; the next, two feet of air separated them.

Two feet of air that felt *very* chilly in comparison to the heat that had just overtaken them.

He watched her narrowly as she touched her fingers to her face. She looked disoriented. She turned her back to him, and then belatedly realized her dress was gaping open all the way to the top of her buttocks. She hastily zipped it up as far as her reach allowed. He watched as the two sexy dimples on either side of the base of her spine and an expanse of golden, smooth, naked back disappeared behind fabric.

He sprawled back on the couch, disappointment and frustration slicing through him like a knife.

"Colleen—"

"Is that why you came over here? Because Mari told you the kids were at my mom's? Because you knew I was alone?" she asked, refusing to look at him.

He gave a frustrated sigh and brushed the long bangs off his forehead. He had a feeling he knew where this line of questioning was going. "I came over here because I wanted to see you. I'm interested in you. It's not a criminal offense that I'd like to have you to myself for once."

"My children *are* usually with me. We're kind of a package deal," she snapped.

"Don't try to make me into the bad guy again," he stated bluntly, leaning forward. "I like your kids, too. That doesn't mean being alone with you doesn't have its unique appeal." He studied her averted profile. His heart sunk a little when he realized the full extent of her vulnerability in that moment.

Damn.

He stood. She glanced back nervously. He held out his arms.

"Come here," he encouraged.

"No," she blurted out. "Don't say anything else. I'm…I'm confused enough." She took another step away from him. "I don't know where that came from," she said, gesturing to the location where they'd just been locked together in a fevered embrace.

"Yes, you do," he said gently. "The same place it came from on Sunset Beach, or in my office the other day. I want you. It's been driving me crazy spending all this time with you for the past week and not touching you. You want me, too."

"I don't—"

"Why can't you admit it's true?"

"Because I don't *want* it to be true," she returned, spinning to face him, her expression a little wild. For a few seconds, they just stared at one another.

"*Is* it because of Darin?" he asked. He glanced at the photo of the smiling man on the mantle. For the first time since he'd noticed the picture, he felt a sharp stab of jealousy.

She straightened and stepped farther away from him.

"Yes," she said shakily.

"I'm not so sure I believe you."

He expected her to whip around again and let him have it in typical Colleen fashion, but she didn't speak. Her silence worried him. It worried him a lot. She stood with her back to him, her forearms wrapped below her breasts, her head lowered. She looked much smaller to him in that moment than he was accustomed to seeing indomitable, vibrant Colleen.

He really was a jerk.

"I'm sorry. Of course I believe you," he said. When she didn't respond, but remained with her head lowered, he sighed. "I'll let myself out."

"I'm the one who is sorry, for sending you mixed messages," she said. "And you're right. I'm not so sure you should believe me about Darin, either. I do miss him, don't get me wrong. But…that's not why I stopped just now," she said in a small voice. She glanced up at him hesitantly, her lost expression killing him a little.

"But believe *this,* Eric. I'm not ready for this. I'm not ready for you," she said quietly.

He watched, filled with regret, as two tears rolled down her cheek. The vision of her filled him…her uncertainty, her vulnerability, her sadness. He lifted his hand and dried the soft, smooth surface of her skin with his thumb, wishing he could do more.

"I'll leave you alone, if that's what you want right now. But I'll see you the day after tomorrow," he murmured, dropping his hand even though he wanted to keep touching her.

"What?" she asked, looking bewildered, tears about to spill from her lovely eyes in earnest. He experienced an overwhelming urge to hold her. He was used to physically connecting with a woman, but this added desire to be tender, to soothe…to make everything better confused him a little.

He took a step toward the hallway, recognizing she needed distance, but never wanting to grant it less.

"We're meeting at the bakery with Liam and Natalie. To choose a wedding cake design," he said.

"But…you don't need to come to that, Eric," she scolded almost fondly.

He smiled, relishing the sound of his name on her tongue. Funny, how such a little thing could bring him pleasure. What had happened to him? When had he become pleased by so little when it came to a woman?

But it wasn't a little thing. Not when it came to Colleen.

"Natalie asked me to meet you guys. I told her I'd come," he replied quickly. In fact, Natalie had casually asked him if he was coming with them to the bakery, but she hadn't seemed particularly invested in whether he was there one way or another. The only thing he knew about cake was that if it tasted good, he'd eat it. The appeal of the cake-choosing ritual rose considerably in his estimation, however, when he learned Colleen would be there.

Another tear spilled down her cheek.

"Colleen?"

"Yes?"

"I meant it when I said you were beautiful."

She started in surprise and then averted her face, swiping at her cheeks with the back of her hand. "My mascara is probably smearing," she mumbled uncomfortably.

He smiled. "It is. And I still mean it."

More than I did even a few minutes ago. You're getting more beautiful by the second in my eyes.

His brow furrowed when he recognized the automatic thought. When had his feelings for her grown so potent?

"I'll see you on Monday," he said gruffly. When she gave him an uncertain nod, he walked down the hallway, leaving her with extreme reluctance.

Chapter Six

Colleen rushed into Celino's Bakery Monday evening carrying a bag filled with Halloween candy. Celino's was in the same strip mall as the Shop and Save. She'd hoped she'd be able to check off two errands in one sweep, but hadn't figured on everyone in Harbor Town having the same idea about getting their Halloween supplies. Now she was late.

The friendly young woman at the front counter immediately showed her to a back room. She paused on the threshold at the vision of Eric inserting a fork and a generous hunk of white cake between his lips. Lined up in front of him on the table were several plates, a slice of cake on each one. Natalie and Liam sat across from him. When they turned to greet her, Colleen saw they were looking through a book filled with photographs of elaborate wedding cakes. A smiling, gray-haired lady sat at the head of the table.

Eric held her gaze as he chewed his cake. Something about his small smile, or the movements of his slightly whiskered jaw, or the expression in his eyes—like they shared a secret—

immediately made her mind leap to that kiss on Saturday night. She'd kissed him several times now, and on each occasion the experience had felt more intense. It made her a little dumbfounded every time she acknowledged how close she'd come to sleeping with him...even when that had been the last thing she'd planned.

Something had changed that night in her living room. Colleen had been forced to admit to herself the obvious. She was attracted to Eric Reyes. *Very* attracted. Denial of that fact seemed ridiculous, considering what had nearly happened.

Nevertheless, that's precisely what she'd determined she needed to do.

She wasn't looking to be in a relationship, and based on Eric's playboy reputation, he wasn't interested in anything serious. He'd more than insinuated, in fact, that he didn't believe in long-term, serious relationships, period. He'd broken his share of hearts in Harbor Town in the past few years; that much was certain.

Engaging in a dance of attraction with Eric, given their future family connection, was a certain recipe for disaster. It was inevitable they'd have to spend time together for the next few weeks. She would be friendly and cooperative. Even a little flirting wouldn't be the worst thing on the planet, would it? But that was as far as she'd let it go.

Definitely. Nothing further than casual, surface attraction. End of story.

What she'd said to him Saturday night kept replaying in her mind, making her blush at inopportune moments.

I'm not ready for this. I'm not ready for you.

She'd never been much of a drama queen before. Her little speech struck her as highly embarrassing, given Eric's casual intentions.

She entered the room and set down the bag and her purse, saying hello to everyone around the table and shaking hands with Lily Celino, the matriarch of the family-owned bakery.

"Sorry I'm late," Colleen apologized. "There was a Halloween rush at the grocery store."

"No problem, we just got started," Lily assured her.

"I see you're enjoying yourself. I should have known there was some reason you wanted to come," Colleen commented to Eric archly as he sunk his fork into a slice of red velvet cake. It seemed easiest just to revert back to her typical sarcastic, teasing manner of relating to him. If she gave him the cold shoulder, it might highlight the significance of those steaming minutes in her living room the other night.

He shrugged. "Someone had to be the official taster," he told her, his eyes sweeping over her appreciatively as she came around the table to sit beside him in the only empty chair. Colleen glanced nervously across the table, hoping Liam and Natalie hadn't noticed Eric's warm appraisal. They hadn't. Liam had a bemused expression on his face as he stared at the elaborate cake design, while Natalie and Lily talked animatedly. Colleen glanced sideways at Eric.

"It's good, isn't it?" she asked quietly, referring to the red velvet cake he was sampling. "It's Jenny's favorite. She always asks for it on her birthday."

"She has good taste. It's the best I've tried so far. You were stocking up for Halloween tomorrow?" he asked, nodding at her bag.

"Yep."

"Brendan's none too pleased with me at the moment," Eric admitted as he sunk his fork into the red velvet cake again. "I had to tell him he's not ready to go off the crutches for another week or so. I hated to disappoint him at his appointment today."

"He'll get over it. You know how kids are about Halloween. He can't think of a good costume that will include crutches, that's all."

She was distracted by Natalie turning the photo book toward her and asking her advice on several cake designs.

By the time they were finished, Liam was looking flummoxed by all the sugary female discussion regarding cake. Eric's eyes had grown glassy with boredom—or quite possibly from sugar shock, given all the cake he'd eaten, Colleen thought with amusement. She'd learned from Eric over the past week and a half that he jogged regularly. That must be the reason he could consume the equivalent of half a cake and maintain such a lean, muscular build.

"How complicated can it be?" Colleen heard Liam mumble to Eric as they all stood and Lily ushered them out the door. "It's flour, sugar and eggs. You bake it. You eat it. End of story."

"I'm glad it's so simple from the male perspective," Natalie said, grinning at Colleen as they lingered by the table. She glanced back at the cake book, biting her lower lip uncertainly. "Are you sure the red velvet cake and cream-cheese frosting won't be too trendy?"

"Absolutely not," Colleen assured her. "It's perfect for a Christmas wedding. I've always thought the red velvet was Lily's specialty. Eric voted it as the best cake, as well."

"Wow. You and my brother agreed on something."

"And they say miracles don't occur," Colleen joked.

Natalie glanced at the door. They were now alone in the back room of the bakery.

"You and Eric seem to be getting along very well. I'm so glad to see it," she said quietly.

"He's all right. He doesn't have to be right one hundred percent of the time, like I used to think. It's more like ninety percent."

Natalie laughed. "You must be getting to him. My odds are much worse." Colleen joined her in laughter.

"There's something I've been meaning to ask you, Natalie," she said as she retrieved her purse and bag.

"What?"

Colleen glanced warily toward the empty doorway. Neither Liam nor Eric were within seeing or hearing distance.

"I've been wondering.... Does Eric know what happened last summer?"

"You mean about Lincoln DuBois being Deidre's biological father?" Natalie asked, suddenly solemn. Colleen nodded. "No. I haven't told him." Natalie shrugged, looking uneasy. "I figured it's such a private thing to your family. It's not my place to talk about it with others. Eric has asked Liam about his and Marc's visits to Lake Tahoe to see Deidre, but he's under the impression that DuBois is an old family friend of your mother's, and that since Deidre is a nurse, she's out there helping to take care of him. I haven't corrected him in his understanding of the situation."

Colleen sighed. DuBois was an old family friend of her mother's, all right—such a good, old family friend that they'd created a child together while her mother was still married to Derry. Of course, Derry had erred, as well. The discovery of Derry's infidelity had been why Brigit had turned to DuBois for comfort.

"You're going to be a Kavanaugh soon," Colleen said as she examined the belt on her coat. "And Eric is part of your family. I'd understand it if you felt the need to tell him the truth. It all relates to the crash, after all. It was the reason my dad was so upset that night...why he got so drunk. It relates to your mother's death, and so it relates to Eric, as well. But I'd appreciate it if you didn't get into it with him in the near future...not while we plan for the wedding, anyway."

"Of course, Colleen," Natalie said in a hushed tone. "I'm actually glad you brought it up. I've been wondering where the line is, in this situation. Eric never shared my obsession to understand the truth about what was going on with Derry on the night of the crash...to discover why your father behaved so uncharacteristically. I figured since he hadn't been as curious as I was, I wasn't as obligated to tell him what Liam and I found out."

"He never thought about my dad's motivations as much as you?"

Natalie shook her head.

"Well…there's little doubt that when it comes to grief and trauma, every human being on the planet responds in a different way," Colleen reflected.

"I know there's been a history of friction between Eric and you," Natalie said earnestly. "But I want you to know, he's been beyond a brother to me. He's been a parent. He would do anything for me."

Colleen stepped forward and gave her future sister-in-law a big hug. "Believe it or not, I know. I'd have to be the hugest fool on the planet not to be able to see how much Eric cares about you." She stepped back and gave Natalie a smile. "At one time, I would have just thought it was easy for him, you being as wonderful as you are. Now…I have to admit, some of the goodness *might* be on his side."

She laughed when she saw Natalie's concern. "I'm only kidding, Natalie. Eric deserves a medal of honor for brotherly affection. My heart has been melting in secret. I'll deny it to the end of my days if you ever tell him, though."

They shared a smile and went out to join the men.

She didn't know why, but she didn't want Eric to know about her mother and father and Deidre. She already felt vulnerable enough around him as it was. Sometimes, she got the impression he saw right through her armor to her insecurities…her weaknesses.

It was the combination of her weakness when it came to resolving her past and her weakness for *him* that had her treading like she was on paper-thin ice.

Eric completed the finishing touches on Brendan's bandages while Jenny jumped several inches in the air. She was trying to assess the success of her Halloween costume in the decorative mirror hanging on the wall in his office and coming up a few inches short.

He affixed the bandage and sat back to study his work. He'd originally thought to use only a smidgeon of the fake blood he'd purchased, but Brendan had gleefully encouraged a more liberal dosage.

Jenny, who Eric had dressed as a physician, had complained that people would think she was a very *bad* doctor given her patient's copious bleeding.

"Better hurry," Brendan said anxiously. "My mom will be here any minute. She sounded surprised when I told her to pick us up in your office."

"Was she worried?" Eric asked, interested in how Colleen would respond to the special plan he, Brendan, Jenny and Brigit had cooked up for Halloween.

"No. She trusts you," Brendan said. "She thinks you're the best doctor at the hospital. She just sounded confused about why Jenny and I were at your office."

Eric did a double take in the process of walking across the room. "Best doctor at the hospital?" he asked, stunned. He removed the mirror from the wall and held it at hip level. Jenny grinned widely as she admired herself in her surgeon's outfit. Luckily, Eric knew a very petite female surgeon who had recently shrunk a set of scrubs in the wash. Only minimal safety-pin usage had been required to fit Jenny's wand-thin frame. The fact that she wore several layers of clothes beneath the scrubs helped. "Where did you get the idea your mom thought that?"

"She said so. I heard her telling my aunt Deidre on the phone yesterday," Brendan said matter-of-factly as he sailed across the office on his crutches in order to inspect his costume in the mirror alongside his sister. Eric had seen a lot of kids use crutches, but no one moved more quickly and effortlessly than Brendan.

Eric absorbed this fascinating tidbit of information as the children vied for a central place before the mirror. He wanted to ask more about what Colleen had said about him, but he couldn't figure out how to without seeming obvious.

"It's not very realistic," Brendan said, inspecting the pair of them in the mirror. "Who would believe that a doctor could be so much shorter than her patient?"

"Who would believe that a patient would be bleeding so much when they have such a good doctor?" seven-year-old Jenny responded with admirable quickness.

Eric smiled. He liked Jenny's feistiness. He'd met her last summer at the fundraiser for The Family Center. Jenny had been surprisingly focused and determined on the task of dunking Harbor Town's mayor, Tony Tejada, in the dunking booth, despite the fact that her small arm wasn't quite up to the task of hurling a baseball the full distance required. Tony had agreed nonchalantly when Eric had suggested moving the mark up a few feet to give Jenny a fighting chance. Tony'd paid for underestimating Jenny's resolve and skill. The tall, slender, seemingly delicate girl had felled the mayor on her first attempt at the newly designated mark. She and Eric had shared a satisfied grin as Tony sputtered and thrashed around in the water behind them. When she'd recognized Eric after Brendan's surgery, they'd quickly resumed their budding friendship.

Did he like Jenny because she reminded him so much of her mother, minus the defensiveness? Eric suspected that was part of it. One thing was for certain: Jenny was a force to be reckoned with, just like Colleen.

"Lots of doctors are shorter than their patients. I'd imagine that's typically the case with Dr. Leung, the lady who gave us Jenny's scrubs," Eric told Brendan mildly. "A good surgeon has a strong heart, a quick brain, a sharp eye and a steady hand. I'd say Jenny has all the makings of one."

Brendan gave a big-brother snort at this, but Jenny just

smiled up at Eric proudly. She jumped and hooted in excitement when someone knocked.

"Look at our costumes, Mommy!" she squealed as she flung open the door. "Eric helped us. See? A real stethoscope…and look at my surgeon's pants and shirt and hat and see this here?" She reached into her pocket. "This is one of those things…a *tongue presser*…"

Colleen glanced at him in the middle of Jenny's exuberant demonstration of tongue-depressor use, her aquamarine eyes wide in amazement. She'd obviously just come from work. She looked very lovely, wearing a soft-looking, fuzzy ivory sweater, a skirt and a pair of calf-hugging leather boots. Her briefcase hung on her shoulder and her hair was styled up on her head with a few wisps brushing her cheeks.

"And I'm the patient," Brendan said, grinning. "Eric said if I had to use the crutches, I might as well have them work for me instead of against me."

"He was overenthusiastic with the blood," Eric said as he hung the mirror back on the wall. "But I might have gone a little crazy with the bandages."

Colleen laughed as she examined her son's costume. "You're right. Every square inch of him is bloodied or bandaged." Her gaze met his. Her curving mouth and sparkling eyes made him feel a little…

…warm.

"Mom was in on this, too? She said she dropped them off at your office half an hour ago. How long have you four been planning this little scheme?"

"Just since Brendan's appointment yesterday," Eric replied. "He was so disappointed about not being able to get rid of his crutches before Halloween, I wanted to do something to help."

"Now I don't mind the crutches at all," Brendan said as he flew across the room in order to retrieve his empty candy bag. "Can we go now? It's almost four o'clock. All the good candy will be gone."

"The good candy doesn't disappear in the first minute, Brendan," Colleen remonstrated with a laugh. She shook her head and glanced at Eric. "Thank you for helping them with their costumes. They're fantastic…and so realistic."

"Only if I'm a psycho-doctor," Jenny mumbled darkly as she eyed her bloody patient.

Colleen burst out laughing. Eric caught her eye and grew two degrees hotter. She had an amazing laugh.

"Mom, can we go, please?" Brendan begged.

"Okay," Colleen agreed, her laughter ebbing. "Tell Eric thank-you for all he's done and say goodbye."

"He's coming with us," Jenny said as she charged for the door, Brendan on her heels.

"Yeah, he said we could trick-or-treat near his house on Buena Vista Drive. I'll bet they have the best candy in that neighborhood…."

Brendan's voice faded as he scurried down the hallway. She regarded him silently, all the humor gone from her expression.

"It was his idea to go on Buena Vista Drive, not mine," Eric told her quickly. He was quite certain she was going to pull the old frosty routine with him, as usual, but instead she smiled uncertainly. These occasional displays of her vulnerability were damn near killing him.

"Do you *really* want to come?"

He reached for his jacket. "I can't wait." He spread his hand at the back of her waist, his fingertips caressing slightly. The sweater was every bit as soft as it looked, but he mostly appreciated the feeling of her firm flesh beneath it. He urged her toward the door. For a second or two, she didn't move, but just looked up at him quizzically. Her long, golden bangs spiked sexily around her eyes; there were a thousand points of green and blue and every shade in between in them.

Finally, she shook her head and headed toward the hallway.

Seeing no signs of protest, Eric gladly kept his hand just where it was. He'd never looked forward to trick-or-treating more in his entire life, childhood included.

It was dark by the time they walked back to her car, Brendan's and Jenny's bags stuffed with candy. Children's laughter and the distant "trick or treat" refrain punctuated the autumn night.

Colleen watched Eric as they strolled down Buena Vista Drive. His chin was tilted down as he listened to Brendan's story about a boy at school who'd been bullying some of the smaller kids. The topic had come up when they'd caught a glimpse of said boy—Dave Irkness—trick-or-treating across the street with a group of older kids. She'd never heard Brendan mention Dave before and was a little shocked he had so much to say.

Was he opening up to Eric because he was a good listener, or did Brendan just require a male ear to discuss such a boy-related topic? Her son was close to both Liam and Marc, but her brothers had been unusually busy lately. There hadn't been an opportunity for much one-on-one guy time. At least the kids would be visiting Marc and Mari in Chicago for the Thanksgiving weekend. Hopefully, Brendan could get in a little male bonding with his uncle then.

Even though she felt a little sad her son hadn't felt comfortable broaching the subject of Dave the bully with her, she was impressed with the way Eric handled the interaction. He affirmed Brendan had been smart in the way he'd dealt with things thus far by standing up for the bullied kids without stooping to Dave's level. The few questions he directed toward Brendan assured Colleen that the teachers and administration had recently become aware of Dave's bullying. She'd be sure to follow up quietly in the background with

Brendan's teacher, knowing how much he would hate it if she made a fuss.

"Why don't you guys come inside and warm up? I have something special I want to show you," Eric said, turning toward her and Jenny.

Colleen blinked and glanced toward the sleek, modern structure of wood, fieldstone and glass at the end of the driveway. She hadn't realized where they were while she'd been so focused on overhearing Eric and Brendan's conversation.

"Can we see Eric's house, Mom?" Jenny asked eagerly. A chilly lake breeze whipped past them, rustling the remaining leaves on the trees. Jenny shivered.

"I don't think so, honey," Colleen said, tucking a lock of dislodged pale gold hair back into her daughter's surgeon cap. "It's getting late. We should get home."

"Aw, Mom," Jenny moaned, giving Eric a desperate, pleading glance.

"It'll only take a moment," Eric promised. "I want to show you what I've been working so hard on, burning the midnight oil. It's Liam and Natalie's wedding present. It's kind of a big deal," he said when Colleen gave him a doubtful look.

"We have to see it, if it's for Uncle Liam and Natalie," Brendan said reasonably, as if Colleen would be off her rocker to suggest anything otherwise.

"All right," Colleen agreed with a laugh that disguised her hesitance. Why *did* the idea of entering Eric's home bother her so much?

Eric surprised her, however, by not leading them toward the front door, but instead to a door to the three-car garage. He flipped on the lights.

"There she is," Eric said.

Brendan immediately let out a stunned *wow*. Colleen stepped around Eric in order to see what had delighted Brendan.

"Oh…it's amazing," she muttered, stepping closer to

the mahogany antique boat perched on a trailer. "It's a Gar Wood," she breathed out in admiration, referring to the company that had made the finest custom-made, wooden speedboats in the country. She'd lived in the vicinity of Lake Michigan her whole life, and she came from a family that adored all sorts of water sports—swimming, diving and skiing. She knew a priceless boat when she saw one, and she knew the sleek craft before her not only packed a punch when it came to power, it was a collector's item to boot.

"Yeah…it's a twenty-eight-foot Baby Gar. Originally built in 1929. Very rare. She's named *Lucy*," Eric explained as he fondly ran his hand along the hull. "*Lucy* is a piece of history. Infamous history," he told Jenny, his dark brows twitching sinisterly, "but history nonetheless."

"What did *Lucy* do?" Jenny asked in a whisper, her blue eyes wide.

"She was owned by a cutthroat gang during Prohibition who used her to transport liquor from Canada to Michigan's Upper Peninsula. *Lucy* was so fast, none of the police boats could catch her. Not a one. She became a legend in those parts. Don't get me wrong," Eric told Jenny, who was looking a little wary as she surveyed the sleek craft. "*Lucy* has a heart of gold. It wasn't her fault she was owned by a band of criminals. She became so famous for her quickness and courage, she was acquired by the Mackinaw Island police department after the gang was arrested, and she served the police loyally for fifty years before she was bought by a man named Albert Ravenswood, who restored her to her full former glory, board by board, about fifteen years ago. Then I bought her."

"And you're giving *Lucy* to Uncle Liam and Natalie?" Jenny asked.

"Yep. It's their wedding present. I'm giving *Lucy* six coats of varnish and some antique brass instruments I ordered online. I've been busy making everything extra spiffy for Liam and Natalie's wedding day."

"Wow," Brendan repeated, apparently too stunned to say anything else. He began to circle the boat, and Jenny followed him.

"I was going to put on some Christmas decorations for the special day. I thought it went with the wedding theme...what was it? A Lake Michigan Christmas? Do you think they'll like it?"

Colleen stared at him in amazement, but he seemed entirely genuine in wanting her approval.

"It's a rare piece of art and history. It's a Baby Gar. Are Natalie and Liam going to like it? Are you mad? They're going to *adore* it."

She blinked when he smiled. He looked unabashedly happy at her praise.

"I'm glad you think so," he said as they began to follow the children, circling the boat. "I know the Kavanaughs love all things water-related, and Natalie has always liked boating on Lake Michigan. I thought *Lucy*'d be a nice addition to their new family. What newlywed couple wouldn't want some nights together on the lake under a blanket of stars?"

"Now I'm about to accuse *you* of being the closet romantic."

His eyes gleamed when he glanced at her sideways. "I just thought they'd like it."

"You thought right," Colleen murmured, studying his profile as he fondly inspected the boat. "Are you sure you're going to be able to let *Lucy* go?"

"They might have to pry her out of my hands, but, yeah—I think my better nature will prevail. You wouldn't believe all the effort and drama I went through to get her."

"It's an incredibly generous gift, Eric."

He did a double take. "Do you think it's too much? I never budged from my bottom line. Besides, an investment I'd made happened to turn out really well, so I had a little extra to spare," he said modestly.

Colleen considered before she spoke. She didn't know precisely what a boat like that would have cost, but she was quite sure the price tag would have been astronomical, even with Eric's bargaining and investment prowess. She wondered how Liam would react to be presented with such a generous wedding gift. She glanced into Eric's eyes and saw how concerned he was about her reply.

"I think it's clear how much you love your sister," Colleen said quietly. "I think it's obvious how much you want her to have a happy future." She paused, and they faced one another. "Do I think it's too much? No. I think it's an amazing gift to start them off on their new life together."

"You don't think I'm coming off as an arrogant snob?" he murmured, one raven eyebrow arched.

Colleen had the decency to glance away in embarrassment. It was precisely what she would have thought of his gift a year ago.

"No. I think it's a generous, but also a very personal and heartfelt, gift. The fact that you worked so hard to get it and are putting some of your own labor into it only adds to that. Natalie is lucky to have a brother like you," she finished hoarsely.

"Colleen."

She kept her gaze averted, but something about the resonant timbre of his hushed, deep voice made her heartbeat escalate. That increasingly familiar feeling of longing she'd been experiencing lately chose that moment to swell in her chest.

"Yes?" she asked softly.

"I know *Lucy* is an eyeful, but do you think you could look at me?"

She hesitantly dragged her gaze off the boat to Eric's face.

"I'm sorry for pushing you the other night," he said, his voice barely above a whisper.

"You don't have to apologize. I'm over it."

His mouth twitched at that.

Not that she was staring at his mouth or anything.

"Are you sure there isn't some other reason why you don't want to become involved with me?"

Colleen glanced furtively at the back of the boat. She could hear the children talking excitedly on the other side.

"I told you. I'm not ready to be in a relationship. Besides, haven't we already established that you don't take your relationships seriously anyway?"

He grimaced in obvious frustration and took a step toward her. Her breath caught when he reached for her hand. "Didn't we cover this? I do take it seriously. Very seriously."

For a moment, her entire awareness resided just beneath his thumb stroking her wrist below the ridge of her palm. She blinked, forcing her sluggish brain back to its logical task.

"You take *sex* seriously. I don't want to be in a casual sexual relationship," she whispered.

"You have to give me a chance, Colleen. I'll go at your pace, but you have to let me in, just a little. Maybe it'll become more than just attraction, if you let it."

She rolled her eyes. "You don't really buy that. Not you. Not the Great Disbeliever."

"I'm beginning to really wish we could start this whole thing over again," he grated out between a clenched jaw.

"Well, we can't," she whispered feelingly.

"Sure, we can."

His eyes looked hot. The lines of his face were rigid, making him appear almost fearsome in his determination. She found herself leaning into him, as helpless as a planet feeling the magnetic pull of a burning star.

Chapter Seven

They were interrupted by a shout from Brendan.

"Mom, you gotta see the leather seats...and check out these instruments!" Brendan called ecstatically. The angle of her son's voice made it clear Brendan had somehow boosted himself into the air to look down into the boat.

"Excuse me," Colleen murmured abashedly, extricating her wrist from his hold. Had she really just almost made out with Eric Reyes with her children fifteen feet away? He watched her from beneath a lowered brow. His face looked impassive, but his eyes spoke to her in concise shorthand.

He desired her, and more than a little bit. And Eric Reyes wasn't the type of man to want something more than a little bit and not get it.

She wanted him, as well. She found him more and more attractive every minute she spent with him.

But Colleen knew she wasn't the type of woman to sleep with a man just because she found him attractive. Sexual attraction was nice. Lust was nice. But she was accustomed to more. She really didn't have the energy required for a fling, not with a demanding job and two children to raise.

"I think he's been climbing again. Crutches and all," Colleen said, starting to move around the boat.

Her words seemed to finally break Eric's intensity.

"Brendan, hold on and stay put!" he called loudly as they both hustled around the boat. Sure enough, her son had managed to pull himself onto the trailer and was lying across the side of the boat, his chest and arms out of sight, the padded, blue cover of his bandaged foot waving around in mid-air. Eric fleetly climbed up on the trailer and assisted Brendan back onto solid ground.

Afterward, he invited them inside, saying they could order Chinese food, a plan which her children heartily supported. However, the spell Eric tended to weave around her in intimate moments had been broken. Brendan's little misadventure had reminded her of the risks involved in climbing too high. It was nice to consider the fact that a handsome, smart, virile man like Eric desired her, but she was a practical woman, a mother with a hectic work and family life. And while Eric inspired that bewildering sense of longing inside of her—in spades—Colleen didn't entirely trust that feeling.

Sure, impassioned romance could get you into a heart-thumping, weak-kneed relationship like Marc and Mari or Liam and Natalie shared. But the higher you climbed, the harder you fell when the bad stuff happened…things like rejection, infidelity…death.

Colleen was too wise, too cautious at this point in her adult life to risk climbing too high and exposing her heart to a man like Eric Reyes.

She managed to avoid him for the better part of two weeks. They saw each other at The Family Center and for a few wedding-planning engagements. Colleen was proud, however, that she'd managed to keep her distance from him in an emotional sense.

It hadn't been an easy feat to accomplish, especially since her family seemed increasingly invested in their friendship with Eric. Despite her initial hostility toward him, her mother's regard for him seemed to grow every day. Brigit had taken to seeking out his opinion about a charity she was involved with at the hospital. Between Eric's sound advice in regard to the charity, his relationship to Brigit's future daughter-in-law, his obvious generosity and care in regard to the wedding plans and his excellent treatment of her grandson, he could do no wrong in Brigit's estimation.

Brigit had now asked Colleen—twice—to ask Eric if he'd like to come over for a family dinner. It was starting to set her on edge.

She chatted with him amiably enough during their encounters, making a point not to notice either the awareness in his eyes or how they occasionally flashed with annoyance when she made sure they were never left alone.

She was following her avoidance strategy one Saturday afternoon while Liam, Natalie, Eric and she were meeting at Holy Name Cathedral with the wedding planner and florist. It was a cold, miserable November day. Lake-effect snow was predicted that evening, but currently rain fell heavily on the steeple roof above them.

She and Natalie strolled down the right aisle while the florist pointed out locations for various arrangements. Her attention, though, was on Eric as she watched him talk and laugh with Delores Shaffner in the center aisle. Why had Liam and Natalie seen fit to hire such a pretty young woman as a wedding planner?

And how did Eric always come off so cool while he was flirting so outrageously?

He didn't lean toward Delores, and his eyes didn't look particularly sultry at that moment, but the women's rights activists of the world ought to propose that smirk be made illegal. That little smile could make the smartest of women into a giggling airhead in about two seconds flat. Colleen grimaced like she'd just bitten into something sour when she heard Delores's church-inappropriate shriek of laughter in response to some comment Eric made.

"Do you think Delores is a little…ditzy?" Colleen whispered to Natalie as the florist measured the altar.

Natalie blinked and followed Colleen's gaze. "Not really. She's been very organized and helpful so far, don't you think?"

"That's before her status as a smart, rational woman was revoked by your brother."

"What?" Natalie asked. Colleen was saved the shame of having to repeat her sullen words when Liam walked up the aisle. His dark blond hair was damp, and he was carefully removing a wet, black police-issue raincoat.

"Sorry I'm late," he said, leaning down to kiss Natalie. Natalie brushed some of the raindrops out of his short, tousled hair. Liam smiled and gave her an even more enthusiastic kiss. "Someone got stuck in floodwaters on Route 11," he said a few seconds later. "We just got her out a few minutes ago. It's going to be a mess later, when the temperature drops," he murmured, his forehead pressed against Natalie's. "I have a feeling I'm going to be working for most of the night."

Natalie repressed her obvious disappointment, smiled and started to lead Liam toward the florist, but he paused.

"Is Father Mike around? He's got a two-foot-deep swimming pool in the south parking lot. When it freezes later, it'll be a skating rink. Just wanted to make sure he knew before mass tomorrow. I'll block off the lot for him, if he wants, but I thought I should ask him about it first."

"He was here when we arrived, but he said he had an appointment in his office," Colleen replied.

Liam nodded. Colleen walked toward Eric and Delores as

Natalie and Liam went to consult with the florist. She lifted her chin as she neared the pair, determined to ignore the way Delores looked at Eric like she was considering taking a bite out of him.

Eric glanced up and met her stare. He'd come to their meeting at the church from work and looked carelessly attractive in a pair of brown dress pants, a button-down shirt, a loosened tie and a sport coat, his overcoat slung in the crook of his arm.

"Is everything okay?" he asked her. "I heard Liam say something about flooding and closing the parking lot."

"Yes, you didn't park in the south lot, did you? Liam says it's filling up with water."

He shook his head. "No, I parked in the north lot. Next to you."

"And I parked next to you," Delores said, catching Eric's gaze. "I *love* your car."

Irritation spiked through Colleen at Delores's words, at her prettiness...at her *presence*. "A couple more weddings like this one, and you ought to be driving one like it in no time flat," Eric said.

Delores's laugh was meant to captivate. Much to Colleen's satisfaction, however, Eric's gaze flickered back to her face.

"Are you getting him used to the center aisle of a church, Delores?" she teased lightly, trying to banish her immature annoyance. Eric could flirt with every woman on the planet, for all she cared. What difference should it make to her? "I wouldn't be surprised if he has a phobia toward it—when it comes to weddings, anyway."

"He better get used to it! He's giving Natalie away," Delores said.

"I'm getting used to the idea...slowly."

Colleen arched her brows. "Nice and easy does the trick, I suppose," she said quietly.

She blinked when Delores looped her wrist through the

crook of Eric's bent arm. "Maybe I better walk with you up the aisle a few times. I suspect you're one of those men who requires practice beyond the wedding rehearsal."

Colleen's spine stiffened. Maybe Delores wasn't ditzy, but she definitely had nerve. She had to remind herself that her fantasies about ways to get rid of Delores's insipid smile were highly inappropriate in a place of worship.

"Actually, I think I'll do my practicing in the other direction, if you don't mind," Eric said mildly, turning his head toward the back of the church. "I see Father Mike, and I need to have a word with him about something. Would you mind coming with me?" Eric asked Colleen.

Delores gave an uncomfortable laugh and withdrew her arm. Eric extended his freed hand toward Colleen. He ignored her wariness, of course, and touched the back of her waist when she walked alongside him. She couldn't decide if she wanted to snarl at him for the proprietary gesture or purr in a satisfied manner that he'd touched her so familiarly in front of Delores's narrowed stare.

"What do we have to talk to Father Mike for?" Colleen asked quietly as they approached the back of the church.

"I wanted to ask him about the musical accompaniment for the singer I hired."

She heard the sound of children's voices and realized for the first time that Father Mike wasn't alone. He was escorting her friend, Ellen Rappoport, and Ellen's two children. They paused near the front doors. Ellen was talking earnestly with the elderly priest while her children—Nathan, age eight, and Melanie, age ten—waited for their mother. It must have been Ellen and the kids whom Father Mike had said he needed to meet with in his office earlier, Colleen realized. She and Eric came to a standstill several feet away, not wanting to intrude.

Melanie glanced around her mother and met Colleen's eye.

"Hi!" the girl called, her thin, somber face lighting up with a grin. She immediately walked over to give Colleen a hug.

"Hey, how are you doing?" Colleen responded warmly. It did her heart good to see the girl smile. Melanie and Nathan had seemed so serious and sad since Cody, their adoptive father, had left. "I'm sorry Ellen, Father Mike," she apologized as Ellen, Nathan and Father Mike approached them. "We didn't mean to interrupt. Eric wanted to speak with you, Father."

"We were just finishing up," Father Mike said amiably.

"No problem at all," Ellen assured him, giving Colleen a quick hug. "I'm glad to see you. We haven't spoken since the engagement party. I know I told you before, but you two did a wonderful job with it," Ellen said kindly, including Eric in her glance. "Are you here about Liam's wedding?"

"Yes. We had a meeting with the florist and wedding planner."

Eric hadn't met Ellen's children, so Colleen introduced him. She began catching up with Ellen and the kids while Eric and Father Mike stepped a few feet away and addressed Eric's question. At one point in their chat, Ellen and Nathan became involved in unfastening Nathan's stuck coat zipper. Melanie looked up earnestly at Colleen, the two of them somewhat isolated from the others for a brief moment.

"We were meeting with Father Mike because Dad…Cody, I mean, hasn't been around to see Nathan and me since he moved out," Melanie told Colleen in a hushed tone.

A rush of compassion went through her when she saw the girl's careworn expression. Melanie was an especially bright girl who seemed older than her ten years.

"That's a good idea for you three to talk to someone. I'll bet Cody's leaving is making you and Nathan really sad."

"Nathan won't say it out loud, but I can tell it's really bothering him."

"And you?" Colleen prompted softly. Melanie nodded in agreement.

"Did it help, talking to Father Mike?"

"Yeah. I was starting to feel…you know, really bad about myself because both my father and Cody left. I thought maybe it was something I did…something about me. But my mom said no way. Father Mike told me that love from parents is very, very important. He said God would never stop loving me for a second, and neither would my mom. He said that the real challenge was for me to keep on loving myself, no matter what difficult things happened to me in life."

"He's a smart man, Father Mike. You're a smart girl with your own unique gifts to give the world. Life will go on, Melanie. You'll see." She ruffled Melanie's hair as they shared a meaningful glance. Colleen's head turned when Eric stepped beside her. He did a double take.

"Are you okay?" he asked, looking confused and concerned as he focused on Colleen's face.

"Of course," she answered, suddenly feeling self-conscious under Eric's stare. He must have read the compassion and sympathy she'd been experiencing for Melanie. He really was a mind reader.

"So, Melanie, when might be a good time over the holidays for your mom and me to take all you kids to the indoor water park?" Colleen asked, neatly turning the subject. She felt Eric's gaze on her intermittently for the next few minutes as their small party was joined by Liam, Natalie and Delores.

She should have known she couldn't avoid Eric for long, however. He called out to her after they'd finished their business in the church and she was on her way to her car.

In his typical fashion, he didn't bother with chit-chat before he cut to the chase.

"What was that all about with Melanie Rappoport?" Eric added as he caught up to her in the parking lot. The temperature had dropped enough so that vapor clung around their mouths. The earlier rain and sleet had turned to fat snowflakes that flurried around them. They paused next to their cars.

"Melanie?" Colleen asked, tightening the belt of her coat. "Oh—we were just talking about life going on after Cody's departure."

"You seemed upset," Eric said.

She shrugged and avoided his searching stare. "What can I say? I like Melanie. It's hard to think about what she must be going through, having not one but two fathers leave her."

He didn't respond immediately. "I see," he finally said gruffly. Colleen studied him from beneath a lowered brow.

"Do you?"

"Yes."

Colleen blinked in surprise, caught off guard by his uncharacteristic irritation.

"I'm not that shallow, Colleen. Cody's misbehavior broke more than just Ellen's heart. I'm not close to them, like you are, but believe it or not I have some inkling how hard it must be for those children...some tiny glimmering of compassion in this robot brain of mine."

"Eric, I'm sorry," she said hastily, feeling contrite. "Of course you do. I didn't mean to imply otherwise."

He shrugged, his shoulders looking especially broad in his overcoat. "It's okay," he muttered under his breath.

"Is there something else wrong?" she asked when he didn't say anything else, just stared at the parking-lot overhead light thoughtfully.

"I wanted to tell you—your mother asked me to join the family for Thanksgiving dinner at her house," he said in a rush, as though he'd been waiting to tell her this news and wanted to get it over with. "I told her I already had plans."

"She *did?* You do?" His revelation was news to her. Why hadn't her mother mentioned it? Why was Eric acting so brusquely all of a sudden? Who were his plans with? Some adoring female, like Delores?

"I told your mother I had other plans, because I knew you wouldn't want me there."

"Oh," Colleen uttered, stunned. She stifled a wild urge to tell him she did want him there, very much. But how could she sound so enthusiastic when she'd spent the better part of the last two weeks making sure they weren't alone? She shivered and dug her gloved hands in her coat pockets, stalling for time while she thought out this little dilemma.

"Do you really have other plans?" she asked him.

"Sure," he said. Her heart sank in disappointment.

"What are they?" she asked, not sure she really wanted to know.

"They're pretty loose at this point, but they might include a TV dinner and football on the tube," he said solemnly.

Sympathy and concern swamped her until she saw the gleam in his eyes and the hint of a smile shaping his lips. "You're pulling at my heartstrings, Tiny Tim."

He laughed, the sound striking her as warm and delicious, ringing in the frigid night air. She chuckled along with him.

"You should come," she said, suddenly sure. "Natalie will be there. It wouldn't be right if we stole your only family away from you on the holidays. Think how unhappy Natalie would be, knowing you were alone on Thanksgiving."

"I'll be perfectly fine eating alone on Thanksgiving," he told her, and he seemed to mean it this time. "I was just kidding before. I'm actually working for most of the day."

"Mom doesn't serve her Thanksgiving meal until the evening."

"The meal schedule isn't really my point." He pinned her with his stare. "You wouldn't want me there. You're avoiding me."

"No, I haven't been—" she began, but he interrupted her.

"You don't have to deny it," he said. The parking-lot light cast enough luminescence that she made out his small, wry grin. "I'd be an idiot not to notice, and I understand why you're doing it."

"It's good one of us does," she mumbled, feeling guilty

for making her cowardly avoidance so obvious. She wasn't sure he'd heard her, because he continued.

"I'm just telling you all this because I wanted to let you know you don't have to be uncomfortable anymore. We have to be around each other for the next month or so. It's unavoidable. But there's no need for you to bend over backward to make sure we're never alone together. I know when a woman isn't interested."

Her guilt swelled. "It's not that I'm uninterested—"

"So you *are*?" he segued smoothly.

"Yes. I mean…no," she broke off, trying to find the right words. She noticed a few snowflakes had landed on his arched eyebrows—stark white against black. She resisted an urge to brush them away. "I think we both know I'm…attracted to you."

"You just don't want it to lead anywhere. I get that."

She made a sound of acute frustration.

"What's wrong?" he asked.

"Eric, do you think you could try not to put words in my mouth for once?"

"I'm sorry," he acquiesced, his lack of argument flustering her even more. "What did you want to say?"

"I'm just confused right now. Maybe it hasn't been right for me to be avoiding you, but I didn't know what else to do," she said in a burst of honesty.

"What are you afraid of?"

She inhaled, trying to stave off the heavy pressure on her chest. Why did this conversation seem so tense…so significant. It wasn't. A guy liked her and she liked him back. It wasn't brain surgery.

"I…" She hesitated, swallowing convulsively. "I told you at the engagement party. I haven't dated in a long time. I'm not really in practice."

"That's good, because I don't like *practiced*. Too predictable. Bores me." He smiled at her droll glance. "I'm interested in you. Not your expertise. Give it a chance, Colleen. Give *me* a chance," he murmured, his voice low and earnest.

"I don't know," she whispered. He dipped his head in order to hear her. She glanced up at him and managed a weak smile. "I'll think about it."

"You will?"

She nodded.

"Will you think about *me?*" His quiet question struck her as highly intimate.

"I can't seem to help it," she admitted grudgingly.

"Good. It's only fair. Between working on *Lucy* and thinking about you, a good night's sleep has become impossible," Eric said gruffly.

She crossed her arms above her waist and stared at the snow falling on the concrete, a strange mixture of pleasure and self-consciousness surging through her at his compliment.

She cleared her throat. "Are you coming to Thanksgiving dinner, then?"

"Are *you* asking me to?"

"Yes," she said, striving for a resolute tone but realizing her voice quavered. She forced herself to look up at him. "I'd like you to come to my mother's house for the holidays. I'd like it very much."

His smile caused her to temporarily forget her anxiety. It was like the sun breaking after a storm.

"Then I wouldn't miss it for the world," he said. He leaned down and kissed her on the cheek. "Good night."

Colleen just stood there, her heart pounding in her chest, as Eric walked toward his car. The kiss had been the height of innocence…friendly, filial, casual.

So why would she have sworn the snowflake that landed where Eric's lips had just been melted into water in a split second?

* * *

She left the parking lot before him. He returned her quick wave as she pulled away. He couldn't help but smile as he backed up a moment later.

Winning Colleen over was a little like handling a skittish colt. Patience was what was required. Rational skill. Subtlety.

But he'd be damned if being logical and methodical had ever been such a grueling challenge in his entire life.

Chapter Eight

The first night of her Thanksgiving vacation, Colleen went to pick up her children at her mother's and found the house empty.

She noticed her mother's car wasn't in her driveway, but still went to the front door. Now that Brendan was a little older, both Brigit and Colleen were comfortable occasionally leaving him in charge while they ran a quick emergency errand. Colleen figured her mother had needed to pop over to the store for a forgotten ingredient for the holiday meal.

But the lights in her mother's graceful, Colonial Revival-style white house were off. The kids must have indeed gone with Brigit. Surely there was a message on her cell phone, Colleen thought as she rummaged in her bag.

There were no messages or texts, however. She was in the process of dialing her mother's number when she saw a piece of yellow paper caught on the porch railing. She leaned down to pick it up and recognized her mother's neat handwriting.

The brisk autumn wind must have whipped it off the door, where her mother usually left notes when she went out.

> *Colleen,*
> *I tried to call you at work, but you were in session.*
> *Meet the kids and me at Eric Reyes's house.*
> *Mom*

Her eyes widened. The kids were at Eric's house? Her *mother* was at Eric's house? She walked to her car, her nerves suddenly jumping with excitement and wariness at once. Thoughts and worries started coming with the rapidity of machine-gun fire. She wasn't sure it was a good idea for her children to become so attached to Eric. The image of Melanie Rappoport's wan face as she told Colleen about her adoptive father abandoning them sprang into her mind.

Don't be paranoid, Colleen scolded herself. She and Eric hadn't even gone on a date, and she was already jumping to marriage, divorce and abandonment.

Other worries rushed in to replace that one. At last, she was being forced to confront her negative attitude about Eric's expensive home. Of course her emotions were all tied up in the usually unspoken knowledge that Eric's status was at least partially a result of her father's fatal mistake sixteen years ago. That night, the fortunes of both the Kavanaughs and Reyeses had been altered drastically, and not just in a financial sense. Both families had suffered extreme loss and grief.

But it was foolish to deny that Eric's house on a beach where Colleen was now banned by law symbolized the Kavanaughs' fall from grace. Maybe most people wouldn't see things that way, but Colleen admitted to herself on that drive over to Eric's that it was precisely what she'd been thinking in some vague, unformed fashion.

She recalled Liam's incendiary words toward Eric in the

parking lot of Jake's Place about Buena Vista Drive two summers ago.

What's the matter, Reyes? Worried about bruising those delicate surgeon's hands? Why don't you just hurry back to that slick house on Buena Vista Drive that my mom's money paid for?

Colleen winced at the memory. At the time, she'd wholeheartedly agreed with Liam's taunt. She felt differently now. Very differently.

Pulling into Eric's driveway, she turned off the engine dispiritedly. She sat in the car, thinking as she stared at the lovely lakefront home.

Was she *jealous* of Eric Reyes?

She cringed at the thought. His mother had been killed. He'd worked his butt off in order to support himself and his injured eleven-year-old sister. They'd been young, alone and essentially penniless, orphans with nothing but their brains and a willingness to work hard. But Eric hadn't just done what it took to make Natalie and him survive. They'd thrived.

How shallow could she be to envy him because of his lifestyle? He'd earned every bit of his right to live in this lovely home, to buy his sister a luxurious wedding gift, to occasionally show the staff at The Family Center his appreciation with an expensive catered meal. She knew how smart he was, and not just in his job as a physician. He'd alluded to the fact that he'd done well for himself with investments. In this economy, that showed some real guts and savvy. His financial status might indirectly be related to Derry Kavanaugh's actions, but Colleen was suddenly sure that the young, intense, hardworking young man she'd known so long ago would have found a way to make a success of his life no matter what had happened to him when he was eighteen.

No…it wasn't jealousy, what she felt toward Eric. It was something more elemental. It was shame. She'd been putting Eric down in her mind all these years in order to make herself feel better. It was easier to think of him being pompous and arrogant than to face her own guilt, anger and sadness about what her father had done; more comfortable to condemn him than to face how helpless and lost she'd felt as a teenager after the crash.

The profound realization of her selfishness hurt. Colleen was used to being the selfless one with her kids, her family and patients. Tears welled in her eyes.

She was so lost in her turbulent emotions, she didn't notice anyone approaching and jumped when someone tapped on her passenger window. Her eyes went wide in shock, tears spilling down her cheek when she saw Eric himself through the glass. He peered at her through the window, his facial features tight with puzzlement that quickly morphed into concern. He wore jeans, a white T-shirt and a blue flannel shirt over it. She hadn't seen him in work clothes since he was a teenager laboring for the landscaping business. Memories of her adolescent admiration of him swamped her consciousness.

"Are you okay?" he asked, his deep voice muffled by the door.

Colleen blinked, and the memory faded. The adult version of that young man looked at her through the window, even more vibrant and compelling than the boy had been. She just nodded helplessly and swiped at a tear.

The next thing she knew, he was opening the car door and sitting in the passenger seat. He mumbled a curse when his long legs wouldn't fit in the compact car, causing Colleen to grin despite her tears. He moved the seat back and slammed the door shut.

"Where are the kids?" she asked.

"Don't worry. Your mom is with them in the garage. They're working on the boat. Brendan dropped by my office last week after a P.T. session and asked if he could help with *Lucy,* and of course Jenny had to come once she heard."

She stared at him in amazement. "Was anyone going to bother to tell me?"

"We did. This evening is the first time they've come. Why are you crying?" he changed subjects abruptly, leaning toward her.

Colleen stared through the front window.

"I always seem to be crying around you," she mumbled. "I hope you'll take my word for it that I don't normally go to tears at the drop of a hat."

"Does that mean the tears have something to do with me?"

She inhaled slowly and sighed. "Inadvertently, maybe," she admitted. She avoided his laserlike stare, but she felt it like a touch on her cheek. "To be honest, I was sitting out here in the driveway trying to figure out why I'm so defensive about going into your house."

"My *house?*" he asked flatly, clearly not understanding.

Colleen sniffed and nodded.

He made a frustrated sound and turned. He grabbed a box of tissues from the backseat. "Here," he said, offering her the box.

"Thanks," Colleen murmured, taking one

"So, what's my house got to do with anything?" he asked after she'd dried her cheeks.

"The house is really just a symbol of it all, I guess. The truth is…" She paused while she withdrew another tissue and dabbed at another falling tear. She felt so ashamed of her idiocy. She could be stubborn at times, but once she'd taken ownership of her failings, her contrition was absolute. Still, this wasn't easy.

"I…I owe you a huge apology," she began falteringly. "I've held so much anger toward you in the past. I've been so unfair. You never did anything to deserve my attitude."

"I may have been stubborn a time or two myself," he admitted sheepishly.

She turned to him and smiled. She *really* liked him in that moment.

"No. You've been nothing but kind and generous ever since Brendan's surgery. I wish you'd accept my apology for being so...prickly around you," she finished in a quavering whisper.

His expression hardened and his eyes widened slightly, as if he wasn't really sure how to take her shift in demeanor.

"Colleen," he muttered. He touched her jaw. His fingers felt pleasantly cool and dry next to her skin. His hand shifted and he palmed her neck, his fingers rubbing just below her scalp. Her entire body stilled in awareness, as if every cell had just gone on high alert at his touch. "If it makes you feel any better, I always understood why you felt the need to go on the defensive around me."

"You did?" Part of her was surprised by his admission, but most of her was completely focused on his massaging fingertips on her nape.

"The cards were stacked against us. Our history saw to that. It was inevitable things were going to be prickly between us, as you put it."

She lowered her gaze, staring at his nose. "Then Sunset Beach happened, and things got even more complicated."

He made a sound of agreement and bent his head toward her. He continued to stroke her muscles with talented fingertips. "I probably should admit that I was attracted to you before what happened there...before the accident, even."

Her gaze bounced up to his. "You were?"

"One time when I was a teenager, I saw you in front of the library. You smiled at me and said hi."

"You remember that?" she blurted out, amazed.

His arched his eyebrows incredulously. "Are you kidding? I was an outsider looking into your world. In the summers, I worked fifty...sixty hours a week. In the hockey off-season,

I was a geek who spent whatever spare time he had with his nose buried in a book—"

"You were not a geek. You were brilliant," Colleen insisted, but he continued as if she hadn't interrupted him.

"One day I unexpectedly come face-to-face with a bunch of pretty girls as I'm leaving the library loaded down with books, and I'm sweating it big-time, and suddenly the prettiest one in the pack—Colleen Kavanaugh—smiles at me. I'm surprised I didn't do a header on the pavement."

She snorted with laughter. "You are so full of it."

His gaze narrowed on her smile. "I meant every word," he murmured. "Your smile still gets me, Colleen."

Her lips trembled in anticipation when he leaned forward and placed his mouth on them. He caressed her firmly... sweetly. Somehow, his tender kiss stirred her just as deeply as his ravishing ones. Something swelled inside her, warm and golden. Disappointment flooded her when he leaned back a moment later and studied her with smoldering eyes.

"Maybe we better go inside before I do something we both might regret," he muttered.

"I'm not one hundred percent positive I'd regret it," she whispered.

"If you keep staring at me like that, you're going to find out quick enough."

She smiled. He smiled back, even though the hard glint of arousal remained in his eyes.

Colleen hadn't realized how warm the interior of her car had become until she stepped into the frigid Lake Michigan wind a moment later. Eric held out his hand and led her up the walk. She slid her gloved hand into his.

"You must be freezing," she said apologetically, referring to his coatless state.

He shrugged and hurried her up the stairs and through the front door. Colleen stepped into an attractive, high-ceilinged entryway that included a marble-tiled floor and a rustic, elegant chandelier. He stepped in front of her when she curiously tried to peer farther into the house.

"You're sure you're ready for this?" he asked, placing his hands on her upper arms.

"Seeing your house?" she asked doubtfully. Something about the intensity of his question made her wonder if he'd been asking about something more serious.

A smile tilted his mouth. "For starters."

"Yes, I'm ready."

"Excellent," he murmured. He dipped his head and kissed her again. She could tell he'd meant it to be a chaste kiss, just like in the car. When he felt her step into him, however, seeking out his hardness, his heat, he groaned and deepened the kiss.

So Colleen had no one to blame but herself for the fact that when she greeted her mom and children several minutes later, her cheeks were flushed pink and her pulse throbbed, fast and furious.

Three and a half hours later, Colleen sat on the plush carpet in Eric's family room before a large coffee table littered with the various pieces from a board game, several soda cans and a few candy wrappers, mostly distributed in front of Brendan.

Like the rest of the house, the room where they sat was luxurious, spacious and yet comfortable all at once, a place where it was just as easy to entertain as it was to cuddle up with a book and blanket. Colleen had asked him if he'd hired an interior designer earlier, and he'd said Natalie had orchestrated the decor. Colleen had seen Natalie's darling town house and knew her plans for the beachside cottage she'd soon share with Liam, so she'd not been surprised to hear she was behind the tasteful decor in Eric's home.

A fire crackled cozily in the large fireplace. Eric, Colleen, Brendan and Brigit each sat one side of the coffee table, engaged in a heated contest of Trivial Pursuit. Brendan and

Eric were beating Colleen and her mother hands down, but the ladies were not accepting defeat easily. During the commercials of her favorite television show, Jenny came over to ask about the score and join temporary forces with the female contingent.

They'd all worked on the boat for several hours together. Eric had already done the strenuous task of stripping the old varnish, so Brigit, Colleen and Jenny had laid on the first new coat of varnish. Meanwhile, Brendan had helped Eric with the task of affixing some of the new brass railings and hardware.

Lucy was looking very pretty indeed by the time they all trooped tiredly into Eric's house for pizza. It'd been fun during dinner, talking about the work they'd accomplished and speculating on how Liam and Natalie would respond when they were presented with the priceless antique boat. The hard work and camaraderie had invested them all in *Lucy*'s makeover.

Colleen fiddled with her empty diet soda can and watched as Eric and Brendan conferred over their question from the Science & Nature category. She was quite sure Eric knew the answer, but as he had for most of the questions, he encouraged Brendan to come to an educated guess on the correct one. It was surprising how much a sixth grader had learned already about science, and even more amazing how well he could divine the correct answer when guided to it by a sharp, brilliant mind like Eric's.

Brendan flushed in pleasure a moment later when his reply to the question won them the game. Colleen smiled broadly as she watched the opposing team celebrate with a fist pump and many self-congratulations. She glanced aside and saw her mother watching her with pointed interest.

She ducked her head, hiding her embarrassment. She and her mother were close. Colleen had been the only Kavanaugh child to choose Harbor Town as her permanent home after she'd married. She'd never admitted it to anyone, but part of her longing to settle in the quaint lakeside community had been her concern for Brigit, living all alone in the large, rambling house in a town where citizens were still known to look down their noses at her due to Derry's actions. Her mother had played a vital role in raising Brendan and Jenny. Colleen didn't know what she would have done without her.

And of course, her mother was a sharp, observant woman. It was no wonder she'd noticed her daughter's admiring glances at Eric.

Brigit stood from the caramel leather couch and stretched. "I'm beat—in more ways that one," she said, winking at her grandson. "I'd better get home and rest, or else we might have pizza for Thanksgiving dinner, too."

Colleen also stood from her position on the floor. "I'll be over in the morning just as soon as I can rouse this crew out of bed," she said, nodding toward the kids. She always went over in the morning to help prepare the Thanksgiving feast.

Brigit nodded. "No hurry. Marc said they wouldn't get there until around noon."

"Can Grandma bring us over after we get back from Chicago to work on *Lucy* again?" Brendan asked Eric.

"I'll take any help I can get," Eric replied.

"Can we, Grandma?"

"Sure, if it's all right with your mother," Brigit said. Colleen became aware that everyone was staring at her. Eric's gaze might have been the most interested of all. Nervousness flickered in her belly. Was it really wise to allow her children to get involved so early, when she'd just decided to attempt the risky adventure of seeing Eric?

"Mom? Can we?" Brendan prodded.

She smiled. "It's fine with me. As long as I get to help, too."

What choice did she have, really? Eric was becoming

part of the family. It wasn't just because of Colleen that he'd become friends with her children.

"Yes," Brendan said triumphantly before he wandered off to see what was happening on Jenny's show. His bandages had been removed a week ago, and much to Colleen's relief, her son was now walking without a limp or experiencing any pain.

After her mother left, Colleen helped Eric clean up the mess from the living room while the kids became absorbed in another television show. When she entered the large, modern kitchen carrying several soda cans, she was highly aware that he was just behind her. Ever since what had happened in the car earlier, she felt both more comfortable around him and more hyperaware of him at once.

She smiled as he tossed a handful of candy wrappers into the garbage. "The last of his Halloween spoils. At least I hope so."

"I'm glad I'm his orthopedic surgeon and not his dentist."

Colleen snorted with laughter and turned to the sink, prepared to clean up the few dishes they'd used during dinner. Eric caught her hand, halting her. She turned to him in surprise. His expression was somber as he studied her, but as usual, his eyes were warm as they moved over her face. He reached for her other hand. He held both next to his legs. Her knuckles pressed against his outer thighs. Since when could the sensation of hard male muscle beneath jeans seem like the height of eroticism?

She really needed to get a life.

"Brendan told me that he and Jenny are spending the holiday weekend in Chicago," he said quietly.

She blinked, the seemingly innocuous statement striking her as charged. "They always go visit Marc after Thanksgiving," she said, perhaps a little defensively.

A small smile pulled at his mouth. Her lips trembled. She

stared fixedly at his collar as he dipped his head and spoke next to her ear.

"I know you weren't sending the kids away with any illicit purpose in mind," he said. "But it is a good time."

"It is?" she whispered. His face was only inches from hers. He possessed a Grecian nose—straight and bold. For some reason, the combination of his nose, his mouth, cleft chin and jaw were nearly as compelling as his dark eyes. Her gaze was often drawn downward...especially when he stood this close.

He nodded and released one of her hands. He used it to brush a tendril of hair off her cheek. She shivered at his light touch.

"Yeah. For us to go out."

"Go out?"

"Yeah...on a date? Friday night?"

She blinked. The thick sexual tension she'd been experiencing fractured slightly. The word *date* sounded a little mundane. Every sense organ seemed to go on high alert at Eric's touch. Her body, at least, seemed to want much more than just a *date* with Eric Reyes. "Oh...a date. Like the movies?"

"Uh-huh," he murmured before he brushed his warm, firm lips against hers. Her body went on red alert once again. He kissed her cheekbone and spoke near her right ear. His breath against her skin made her tingle with delight. It reminded her she was alive...an exciting, vibrant woman.

"I pick you up, we go to dinner and a movie, we talk. A date."

"A date," she repeated, as if she'd never heard the word in her life. It took on a whole new meaning when Eric said it. "Okay."

He leaned back slightly and smiled. "Yeah?"

She nodded and stared up at him, transfixed, her desire swelling. Then she freed her hand and grasped his shoulders. She went up on her toes and touched her lips to his.

She kissed him like she meant it, and when Colleen threw herself into something, she made it count.

When they separated a moment later, both of them were breathing heavy. Eric looked like she'd just hauled back and clobbered him with a club.

"That means you *do* want more, right?" Something akin to bliss was starting to filter into his dazed expression.

She gave him a droll glance and kissed him once more on the mouth. "I think that's been pretty well established," she said, removing her hands from his shoulders with reluctance. "I'll think about it in a rational manner and give you my final decision on the matter tomorrow evening after dinner."

He looked like she'd just clubbed him again. *"Rational manner? Final decision?* You're starting to make me nervous. Is this some kind of a test?"

"Don't be ridiculous," she chastised, extricating herself from his arms. "I should go. I've got to get the kids to bed."

"Colleen," he said darkly when she started to sweep past him.

"I'm not trying to be difficult," she said, taking in his rigid expression.

"I want you so much I can't sleep at night. And you're telling me you plan on putting me on trial while you make a rational decision?"

"It's not a trial."

"After everything that's happened tonight—after the way you just kissed me—how can you even say the word *rational?*"

Her spine stiffened. It was hard enough for her to walk away from him, to focus on the mundane details of her life, when all she wanted to do was throw herself back in his arms and allow him to sweep her away on a tidal wave of sensual delight. It frustrated her that she couldn't express adequately to him how daunting this little adventure was for her. It might be run-of-the-mill for him to woo a woman, but Colleen felt like she was stumbling around clumsily in new territory. The knowledge of her vulnerability set her a little on edge.

"What's the problem, Eric? Aren't you the banner-waver for the 'let's be rational about romance' society?" she asked in a hushed voice.

Something shifted in his expression. "So you want to be rational?' he asked, his calm tone belying the hard glitter in his gaze. "All right. Good luck."

"What's that supposed to mean?" she asked warily.

"Just that I've tried it," he muttered through a tight jaw, his low voice rough with emotion. "I've succeeded at being objective my whole life." He startled her by reaching up and cupping the side of her neck in his palm. "Only problem is, it doesn't seem to be working all that well when it comes to you. If I can't be logical about this, I hope to hell you can."

He leaned down and kissed her, hard, quick and potent. Thought evacuated her brain. Her toes curled in her boots. A few seconds later, he released her and walked out of the kitchen, leaving her to her chaotic thoughts and a body buzzing with arousal.

His admission that he was having difficulty in maintaining his objectivity when it came to her left her stunned. It was so unlike him to be so forthright...so transparent. Wasn't it? she wondered, her confusion mounting.

Damn that man, she thought heatedly as she smoothed her hair and tried to pull herself together.

How was it that he always managed to get in the final word?

Chapter Nine

A plate crashed onto the floor, causing Colleen to squeak in surprise. She set down the tray of china she'd been carrying on the kitchen counter and knelt to retrieve the jagged pieces.

"Be careful, honey. Don't cut yourself," Brigit advised from where she stood next to the oven, a whisk poised in her hand.

"I'm sorry, Mom," Colleen moaned in regret.

"It's okay. It's not like it's precious china or anything." Colleen met her mother's blue eyes and saw she was teasing. Brigit set down the whisk and stretched out her hand. She pulled Colleen up to a standing position.

"You stir the sauce. I'll clean that up," she said, bustling toward the pantry. "It was just a salad plate. I've got plenty extra of those."

Colleen stood at the stove, feeling clumsy and out of sorts, when she heard the broken china clinking in the garbage a moment later.

"Now," Brigit said as she opened up the refrigerator and

withdrew a casserole dish, her movements economical and graceful. "How about if you rinse off the china, and I'll take over at the stove?"

"Are you sure you trust me with it?" Colleen muttered.

"Quite sure," Brigit said breezily. "And while you're at it, why not tell me what's got you so distracted today? Or should I say *who's* got you so distracted?"

Colleen glanced sideways at her mother and sighed. She'd been right last night. Her perceptive mother had picked up the sparks between her and Eric.

"Nervous about Eric coming to dinner?" Brigit asked matter-of-factly.

"A little. Technically speaking, it's the first date I've been on since I was twenty years old," she mumbled morosely. She glanced over at her mother. "Aren't you nervous about Eric coming here?"

"Not so much. A few months ago, I would have thought it was bizarre, the idea of him coming to a family Thanksgiving. I remember how angry he was during the hearings. Sometimes I felt like he thought I was the one who had robbed him of his mother and injured Natalie." Brigit had a faraway look, as if seeing those emotion-filled, painful memories after Derry's death from a great distance. She sighed and turned off the gas burner. "Eric was just a kid at the time. I don't blame him for his anger, even if I had trouble accepting it back then. I was too filled with my own grief, my own loss, to comprehend how another person could hold anger toward me. I didn't understand that when death strikes so many, the emotions ricochet around like a bullet in a sealed room, hitting targets you would never expect. Eric's anger toward me was just as misplaced as mine toward him. It was wrong, but it still makes sense. Maybe we needed to go through it. Maybe. But it's done now."

Colleen stood very still next to the counter, goose bumps

on her arms. Seeing her mother in an unguarded moment was rare.

"You like Eric, don't you?" Brigit asked quietly.

"Yes," she replied, averting her face while she began rinsing the plates.

"What's the problem, then? I see the way he looks at you." Colleen turned her head at the sound of her mother shutting the stove. The delicious aroma of roasted turkey and sweet potatoes wafted through the air. "I can tell you're nervous, honey. You always did get quiet when you were worried about something."

"Quiet and clumsy," Colleen mumbled.

"Exactly."

She knew Brigit wanted her to open up, but she felt torn. How could she tell Brigit that one of the reasons she was feeling so conflicted about engaging in a relationship was her hurt over what she'd discovered about her mother and father? She wasn't a child anymore. It wasn't as if her parents owed her anything.

So why do I feel so betrayed?

Her hands stilled as she set down the gravy bowl. The thought shocked her a little. Is that how she felt? Betrayed by the knowledge of her parents' infidelities?

"I've worried about you," Brigit said, drawing her out of her thoughts.

"Me?" Colleen asked, caught off guard. "Why?"

Brigit took off the oven mitts, looking thoughtful. "For the first couple years after Darin died, I understood you were grieving. I know how hard it was for you. But as time went on, I began to wonder if you'd ever consider allowing other men into your life. You're so independent. You're a lot like me that way."

Colleen continued with her actions, as though nothing was wrong, but Brigit's unexpected openness made the questions she'd been repressing for the past few months pop into her brain.

Why did you do it, Mom? How could two people who loved each other so much have strayed? Part of her was desperate to understand how her mother could have betrayed Derry... how Derry could have betrayed her.

"Colleen," her mother said softly, drawing her out of her thoughts. She went still when she saw Brigit's expression. Her pretty face looked more lined than usual, weighed down by sadness and regret. Dread rose in Colleen's breast. It reminded her of how she'd looked on that night last summer when Liam had confronted her about Lincoln DuBois.

They'd spoken of it on that night—Derry's emotional upset at the time of the crash, Brigit's affair with DuBois and the discovery that Deidre wasn't Derry's child. Brigit had been devastated by revealing those secrets to Colleen and Liam, but Colleen had remained strong, trying her best not to crumble when her mother was so vulnerable.

"Yeah, Mom?" Colleen asked in a false "everything is fine" tone.

"Does any part of your nervousness about Eric have to do with last summer?"

"Of course not," Colleen murmured evenly, her heart thrumming louder in her ears at the knowledge that Brigit had somehow gleaned her private thoughts.

She glanced sideways when her mother didn't immediately respond. Brigit's mouth trembled.

"Because I want you to know something. I know everyone—maybe me most of all—has said you and I are alike over the years, but they're wrong. *I'm* wrong, to always be saying that to you." Brigit inhaled as if for courage. "The truth is, you're stronger than me. I keep things to myself, while you were always comfortable with who you were. You were always confident enough to openly express your emotions."

"Mom—" Colleen began, but her mother stopped her by holding up her hand in a halting gesture.

"Let me just say this, and it'll be done. Mari told me about what you said to Janice Tejada at the engagement party—how Janice should go and talk to Tony while the emotions were fresh...get it all out in the open. I'm not sure how you got so wise about that sort of thing, but you certainly didn't get it from me or your father. We hid our feelings and vulnerabilities...buried our hurt. We paid for it in the end. I can't tell you how proud I am of you for being so open and honest about your feelings."

"Your pride may be misplaced," Colleen said, thinking of her cowardly avoidance of Eric because she didn't know how to handle her attraction to him.

"I don't think so," Brigit said quickly. "Anyway, I won't belabor this. It's still a tender wound for all of us, and it's a holiday. I'm only bringing it up because I know how your mind works. I've seen how you look when you're second-guessing yourself, and you've really got yourself twisted into a knot when it comes to Eric. I just wanted to say, you and I—we're two different women. I made mistakes in regard to love, and I live with that regret. But don't make my regret yours, honey. Try to trust yourself."

A shudder of emotion went through her. "Mom, I don't know what to say."

Brigit smiled and opened up a drawer. "You don't have to say anything. I was the one who needed to do the talking. Now...after you've set the table, would you mind peeling some carrots for the relish tray?"

Colleen accepted the peeler her mother handed her, both relieved and sad their conversation was at an end. "Of course. And Mom?"

Brigit paused in walking toward the stove and glanced back.

"I know we're completely different people. But I've always been proud to be compared to you."

Brigit's lips trembled. She came over and gave Colleen a quick but heartfelt hug before she resumed her cooking, averting her face. Colleen noticed her surreptitiously wiping at her cheek with her apron. Poor Mom. *Always so protective of her feelings,* Colleen thought with a bittersweet mixture of fondness and sadness.

What her mother had said was true. They were very different women, but Colleen loved Brigit—imperfections, mistakes and all—just the same.

Brigit's unexpected insight and advice had made Colleen feel a little less burdened by her worries. Nevertheless, when she heard the doorbell ring at six o'clock sharp that evening, her heart began to flutter erratically.

"That's Eric. I'll get it," Natalie said, closing the refrigerator door. She'd come a few hours early in order to help with the cooking. Liam, Marc and Mari were already there, watching football in the family room with the kids.

"No, that's all right," Colleen said breathlessly. "He's my guest. I'll get it."

Natalie paused in mid-stride, her eyes going wide.

"I…I hadn't realized. That's wonderful."

Colleen gave her a smile—albeit a nervous one—and headed toward the front door. Before she answered it, she hurriedly tossed off the flats she'd been wearing while she cooked and slid on the heels she'd brought.

He stood on the front porch, looking very handsome in a dark blue overcoat, a starkly white shirt and a conservative black, white and burgundy print silk tie showing above the collar of his coat. In one gloved hand he held a bottle of wine, and in the other he carried a large basket wrapped in plastic. It was tied very artfully in an elaborate bow, making it seem especially frilly given the virile, broad-shouldered man who held it.

She smiled, and he returned it.

"Come in," she said. "You're right on time."

"I wouldn't dare to be late my first time to the Kavanaugh house," he said, glancing at her appreciatively. "You look beautiful."

"Thank you," she replied lightly, even though she was stirred by the earnestness of his tone. She held out her hands for the basket and wine so he could remove his coat. "You came bearing gifts."

"Didn't think it could hurt," he admitted. "There was a time when I was the last person in town your mother would have invited for dinner."

"Well, things change," she said, balancing the enormous basket on her hip.

"Good," Eric growled softly before he kissed her, taking Colleen by surprise.

Pleasant surprise.

His lips were cool on the surface from the chilly November night, but she felt his heat underneath. He smelled like soap and spice—even more delicious than the scents wafting from the kitchen.

She blinked dazedly when he raised his head a moment later. His smile was a little devilish as he fleetly unbuttoned his overcoat.

"Thought I better get that in before family descended," he said, his tone hushed in deference to the sounds of conversing voices, the sports commentary on the football game, excited yelps coming from her niece, Riley, and rattling pans in the distance.

She started to chastise him out of old habit, but caught herself. "Good idea," she said instead. She ceded the large basket to him when he'd hung his coat on the coat rack and his hands were free. "This is absolutely gorgeous," she said, referring to the elaborate basket filled with scrumptious-looking bakery items. "Did you order it from Sultan's?"

"I did. I wanted to look good."

Her glance ran over his tall, fit form garbed in an immaculately cut gray suit, not bothering to hide her admiration. "I have to say, you do a pretty good job of making yourself look good without any help, Dr. Reyes."

His playful expression hardened. Mirth gleamed in his eyes, but so did elemental male desire. A thrill went through her at the sight of it.

"Is that a compliment? From Colleen Kavanaugh?"

She hitched her chin toward the hallway and grinned over her shoulder.

"I do believe it was."

Their opening exchange set a good tone for the rest of the evening. Colleen's nervousness faded when she saw how comfortable both Eric and Natalie seemed at dinner, how every member of her family welcomed the Reyeses. She hadn't quite realized until they sat down for the Thanksgiving feast how integral Eric had become during the past month or so. Everyone had questions for Marc about his big decision to run for the U.S. senate. After that, the topic of conversation turned to Natalie and Liam's wedding. Eric fit right in to the homey family discussion.

Colleen sat between Eric and her niece Riley's high chair, helping Mari feed the energetic nineteen-month-old girl. As they talked about the possibility of Brigit's sister's family coming from Sacramento to attend the wedding, Riley cheerfully threw a bit of sweet potato onto Colleen's cheek.

Colleen's mouth was still open in surprise when Eric said, grinning, "This way."

Colleen turned her cheek to him, and he wiped it with his napkin, pausing to gently push a tendril of hair behind her ear, stroking her temple. It all happened so fast, she didn't have time to be self-conscious about his caress in front of her whole family. When she sat back, she saw everyone had paused and was staring at her and Eric with expressions that ranged from wide-eyed curiosity (Jenny) to pleased (Natalie, Brendan and her mother) to smug (Mari) to stunned (her brothers).

Riley yelped in protest that no one was paying attention to her anymore. Everyone started eating again, while Eric valiantly resumed the topic.

After dinner, everyone helped to clear and clean up while the kids played with Riley in the living room. It was a plan which caused just as much camaraderie as it did chaos as they bumped into each other, the men shouted questions for instructions on what went where and Brigit answered them good-naturedly, then followed behind, silently correcting all their mistakes. When Marc attempted to shove the huge roasting pan in the packed dishwasher, though, Brigit drew the line and shooed everyone out of her kitchen.

Colleen was the last to leave. She wandered down the front hallway and looked into the family room, not seeing the face she sought. She turned her head, hearing the muted sound of men's voices in conversation. The curtained French doors leading to the formal living room were partially opened. A table lamp softly lit the room. She poked her head inside and saw two tall men in their shirtsleeves standing in front of the built-in bookcases.

"What are you two doing?" she asked in a hushed voice.

"Eric was interested in Dad's book collection," Marc said.

Colleen's eyes swept over the large, handsome collection of books and landed on Eric. She smiled.

"Dad loved his books. He didn't have that many growing up. He used to say—"

"There was no greater wealth than knowledge. Marc just told me," Eric said, holding her stare.

"Eric was just talking about Dad when you came in, Colleen. You knew him? Before the crash?" Marc directed his question to Eric. Colleen walked toward the two men, her interest piqued.

"Not really," Eric admitted before he slid a book back into the bookcase and turned toward them. "I knew who he was, though. I worked for Morelli Landscaping when I was a kid. I wasn't assigned to this house—Kevin Little used to do the landscaping and upkeep here—but one spring, Kevin's crew was short one guy, and I filled in. During my breaks, I used to read. That's how Kevin found me one day, under a tree with my nose in a book. Kevin wasn't used to me. He didn't know that I worked like a madman but grabbed a book on my break. He thought I was slacking off and started to lay into me. Next thing I know, I hear someone calling out to Kevin from the front porch. It was your dad. He must have heard us in the yard. He asked to speak to Kevin. I couldn't help but overhear their conversation from where I was sitting."

"Dad told your boss to lay off you, didn't he?" Marc said.

"Yeah. How'd you know?"

"It's what Dad would have done in that situation," Colleen said quietly, sharing a meaningful glance with her eldest brother. "He didn't have much when he was growing up. He believed in the power of hard work and education. He would have been the first to defend a kid reading on his break."

In the distance, they heard Riley start to wail. "All that sugar from dessert has her battery overcharged. I better go assist the troops," Marc said with a smile. He squeezed Colleen's shoulder as he left, confirmation that he'd been as affected by Eric's memory of Derry as she had been.

"Do you want to sit down?" Colleen asked, waving at the sofa. The sound of the French door shutting quietly behind Marc had highlighted the fact that she was alone with Eric.

"He and my mom were alike in that way," Eric said.

"Excuse me?"

"Your dad and my mom," he said. His eyes narrowed thoughtfully as he stared at the bookcases. "Education. Hard work. My mom drilled that into me practically from the day I was born."

Colleen swallowed with effort. It seemed like such a charged topic. "Natalie has told me a lot about your mom. She sounds like she was an amazing woman," she said.

"She was."

The silence and Colleen's discomfort mingled...swelled.

"What's wrong?' Eric asked quietly.

She shook her head and laughed. "It's an old feeling, but it still haunts me at times."

"What's that?"''

"The urge to apologize for my father's actions," she murmured after a pause, studying Eric's hand where it rested on his thigh. "And the subsequent rush of anger...wanting to defend him...wishing like crazy I could...feeling helpless because I know I can't."

He reached out, pulled her toward his body in a comforting gesture. Colleen recalled her earlier conversation with her mother. She glanced into Eric's face. It was shadowed and sober-looking in the dim room.

He rubbed her shoulders with his fingers. It soothed her, his touch...reassured her. "I know that. If I didn't always know it as well as I do right now, I'm sorry."

"It was such a hard thing, the crash...for everyone. Everything was so raw. Emotions just get splattered everywhere in the aftermath, I guess."

"I was so busy tallying up the things your father had stolen from me, I never really paused to think about who he really was, let alone what my life would have been like if the crash hadn't happened." He shrugged. "Who knows? Maybe I wouldn't have had the drive it took to go to college and medical school if there weren't so many barriers just taunting me to leap over them."

Colleen smiled. "And maybe I wouldn't have gotten married in such a rush and started a family so quickly, desperate to create my own little secure world."

He held her stare. "Is that what you think happened?"

She sighed. "Maybe. If that was part of my motivation for an early marriage, I don't regret it. I had a lot of good years with Darin. I have Brendan and Jenny, and who could regret that?"

He nodded in agreement. He shifted his hand, massaging her tense shoulder and neck muscles. She let her head drop onto his chest and inhaled the clean scent of his laundered shirt and the subtle spice of his cologne. Her eyelids grew heavy. It felt so good.

"When you say you miss Darin…"

"Yes?" she asked when he paused, her eyelids still closed. When he didn't immediately respond, she opened her eyes and lifted her head from his chest.

"Forgive me for being curious," he said.

"It's okay," she whispered.

"I was just wondering to what degree Darin is still with us, when I'm alone with you."

The way he'd posed the question had caught her off guard.

"He's not."

She averted her gaze, a little stunned by her outburst of honesty. She realized for the first time just how true it was. When she was with Eric, she was totally absorbed by him, whether he was pricking her temper or kissing her until she couldn't think straight. It wasn't as if he blocked Darin out of her mind. Darin was still there, a warm, happy memory she cherished.

But it was Eric who dominated her thoughts in the present.

"I see," Eric said slowly, although his tone made her think he really didn't *see* at all but was too polite to risk treading on the delicate topic of her dead husband. It wasn't really fair to leave him completely in the dark, always stumbling around, walking on eggshells around her, was it?

"Darin was a wonderful man. He was there for me at a

time in my life when I most needed him. I'll always be thankful for that. He's the only man I've ever been with."

Eric's massaging fingers stilled in the crook of her neck and shoulder. She looked into his face warily. She couldn't believe she'd just said that. It had sort of erupted out of her.

"I thought you should know," she said lamely.

His stunned expression faded. He nodded and resumed massaging her. She curled farther into him, highly aware of his presence, his hardness, his warmth. She found herself fiddling with his silk tie. Her hand strayed to his chest. She stroked him, fascinated by the sensation of hard, corded muscle beneath his dress shirt.

"And that's because you cared so much about him?" he asked in a tone that struck her as deliberately neutral. Or was it strained?

"Of course I cared about Darin, but I don't know if I avoided men since he died because of that or not," she said, feeling a little helpless because she didn't know the answer herself. "I never cared enough for anyone else since Darin died to even think about the topic."

"Colleen..."

"Yes?" she asked, distracted by the feeling of his muscles beneath her fingertips and the way he was staring at her mouth.

"You're killing me. You know that, don't you?"

"I don't mean to."

"I think that might be what's killing me the most," he growled softly before he slid his hand behind her neck and pulled her to him. His mouth covered hers. Colleen melted into his kiss. Everything about him—the feeling of his hard male body, his scent, his taste—delighted her. He knew how to kiss her just the way she liked it—firm and demanding at times, playful and teasing at others, nipping at her lips gently, making her hungry, coaxing her into becoming the aggressor.

He groaned when she did just that, framing his jaw with her hands and sending her tongue into his mouth, submerging herself in his heat and taste.

There was something so elementally *right* about him.

All of her doubts about whether or not it was a mistake to get involved with Eric faded under the power of his kiss and stroking hands. She forgot her worries about the kids and whether or not she was opening them up for hurt by allowing them to get attached to Eric. Her fears about her own vulnerable heart disappeared as desire surged through it, making it pump fast and strong.

"I'm not going to be able to hold out much longer," he mumbled a while later as she plucked at his lips and he held her rib cage in his large, splayed hands. "Did you make your rational decision yet?"

"What?" Colleen asked between feverish kisses.

"Your decision. You know…" He paused and delved his fingers into her long hair. He clutched and tugged back gently, stretching her throat back. She moaned softly in protest because the position prevented her from ravishing his mouth more. Perhaps that was his plan, however, because he proceeded to devour her exposed neck, making her tremble in excitement. "The one about wanting more…with me?"

"Oh," she gasped when his mouth lowered and he kissed the exposed skin on her chest. His hands shifted from her back, cradling her ribs just below the fullness of her breasts. His lips followed the trail of the neckline of her sweater, awakening her nerve endings, making her nipples tighten. Heat flooded her.

"Colleen?" he prompted, lifting his head and spearing her with a smoky stare.

"I…I'm very close to making my decision."

"Good," he muttered. "Let me see if I can't be a bit more persuasive." He dipped his dark head again and resumed tasting her skin. Colleen sighed in pleasure. He lifted his head a moment later and grabbed her hand. He placed it on his chest.

"I liked you touching me," he said. "Do it more. Please."

She acquiesced without hesitation, eager to comply. He leaned toward her again, his gaze fixed hungrily on her mouth, but he paused suddenly, his attention captured by her stroking hand. For some reason, his focused gaze made her all that much more aware of her hand on his chest, her exploration of dense, lean muscle. He leaned back on the couch, and they both watched as her fingertips slid over his right nipple. She explored the tiny, turgid button of flesh, fascinated by the feeling of it through his cotton shirt.

He leaned his head back on the couch and hissed softly. He covered her stroking hand with his own and moved it down over his ribs. She explored the sensations and textures of him there just as enthusiastically, captivated by his focus on her, feeling his heart beating more rapidly beneath her moving hand.

She laid her cheek on his chest and reached between two buttons. He made a rough, muffled sound in his throat when she touched smooth, warm skin. She'd thought he'd move or say something, but instead he remained completely still as she stroked his ribs, as though her touch had put him under a spell. She felt his skin roughen and felt her power over him in every cell of her being.

He put his hand on top of hers and slowly, gently slid it down over his abdomen. His stomach muscles felt taut and delicious beneath her seeking fingers. Her cheek burned hot next to his chest. She slid her fingers into an opening in the shirt just inches from his belt buckle. He groaned as she stroked him, skin to skin.

Her heart stalled when he put his hand on tops of hers yet again.

She lifted her head from his chest and met his stare. An unspoken message seemed to leap between them. Eric gave a small smile and lifted her hand, pressing his mouth to the center of her palm.

Colleen sighed in mixed pleasure and regret when she heard Jenny calling out to her from the stairs.

"Mommy! Did you bring my pillow inside?"

She gave Eric an apologetic glance and sat up straight, extricating herself from his embrace. "She must be getting tired. She can't sleep without her special pillow, even though she'd never admit it out loud."

Warmth surged through her when he chuckled. She was glad he wasn't offended at being interrupted. Besides, as heated as they'd been getting, it was probably best Jenny chose that moment to require her pillow.

"You go ahead," he said gruffly, rubbing her upper arm. "I'll stay here for a moment and...cool down a bit. I should probably get going anyway."

Heat flooded her already flushed cheeks.

"Oh—" She glanced around when Jenny called again, flustered. She shouted toward the closed French doors. "Just a second, honey! Are you sure?" she asked, turning back to Eric.

Eric nodded. "The evening's gone great so far. I don't want to ruin it by having your family catching me mauling you," he said wryly.

"What about if—" But Jenny was knocking on the door, and Colleen stood to open it. She hustled Jenny out to the hallway to give Eric a moment to collect himself. By the time she'd put on her coat and gone out to her car to retrieve the pillow and duffel bags for the kids' trip to Chicago, Eric was standing in the foyer putting on his coat and talking to a sleepy Jenny. Jenny thanked her for her pillow and wandered out of the foyer.

Frustration filled her as she set down the duffel bags and faced Eric. Both of them wore their coats. Marc and Mari must be preparing to leave for Chicago, because the sounds of bustling people and voices sounded close by.

"I had a great time," Eric said in a hushed tone. "Thank you for inviting me."

"You're welcome."

"We're still on for tomorrow night, right?"

"For our date?"

He smiled.

"Of course," she murmured, suddenly feeling ridiculously shy.

"Good." He reached up and brushed back her hair, briefly touching her cheek with a gloved finger. "I already thanked your mother and said goodbye to your family, so I'll say good-night. I'll call you tomorrow."

She nodded. He leaned down and kissed her—brief and electric. Her frustration turned to acute disappointment as she watched him walk out the door. Things weren't turning out exactly the way she'd planned. She wasn't ready to say goodbye to him so soon.

"Mom, did you pack my iPod?" Brendan asked her from the hallway.

Colleen sighed and realigned her brain into Mom mode. "Yes, it's in your duffel bag."

"Good, 'cuz Riley is already asleep, and Jenny is going to be, too, as soon as we get in the car. I'll have to be quiet on the way to Chicago," Brendan mumbled.

Everyone gathered in the hallway and foyer, putting on coats and giving hugs. Colleen solemnly charged her children to do whatever their Uncle Marc and Aunt Mari said, not to sulk and to pick up after themselves. She gave them both some spending money and huge hugs.

"I'll be calling you over the weekend," Mari said when she came to say goodbye. Her significant glance told Colleen loud and clear that Mari wanted the entire scoop about Eric. They hadn't really had a chance to talk privately all day.

"I might be busy," Colleen whispered. Mari's eyes went wide in increased interest before she gave Colleen a hug. Soon Marc, Mari, Riley, Brendan and Jenny were backing out of the driveway, only to be followed by Liam and Natalie. She and her mother stood in the foyer, the overhead light on, waving goodbye.

"Do you want to spend the night here, honey?" Brigit asked after Liam's car had disappeared down Sycamore Avenue.

"No. I can imagine you'd like some alone time, after all the hard work you did. Thanks, Mom. For everything," she added.

She felt strange a few minutes later as she backed out of the driveway. It was odd, not having Brendan and Jenny with her. Yet she didn't feel lonely, necessarily. She felt…excited.

She shivered uncontrollably. The temperature had plummeted and the car heater seemed to be having no effect. It wasn't until she turned left, not right, on Travertine Drive and drove west—in the opposite direction of her house—that she realized she wasn't trembling from cold, but from anxiety.

And excitement.

It took Eric only seconds to answer her knock, but it felt like tortuous minutes to Colleen. The entryway light switched on and the door opened. She froze when she met his gaze through the outer glass door pane. He was wearing only a pair of black sweatpants. A towel hung around his neck. He was swiping one end of it across the damp hair at his nape, a slightly puzzled look on his face.

His expression stiffened when he saw her standing on his front stoop. Her gaze swept down over his naked torso. Moisture gleamed on taut, olive-toned skin.

He dropped the towel and whipped open the door.

"I'm sorry. You were in the shower. I should have called—"

Her apology was cut off short when he reached for her

elbow and drew her into the house. The sound of the door shutting behind her sounded like a gunshot in Colleen's over-sensitive ears.

"You're shivering," he murmured, chafing her back and upper arms. "It's freezing out there." He backed up and started to unfasten her coat. "Come on inside. I'll start a fire."

She laughed. He paused and glanced up at her face, the ends of her belt in his hands.

"What's funny?" he wondered aloud.

She shook her head as if to clear it. "You didn't even ask me what I was doing here."

He resumed unfastening her coat. Colleen tried to ignore the feeling of his long fingers moving down her chest and belly, working the buttons through the holes, but it was difficult. "I guess I was too busy being happy to see you to question why you were." He glanced toward the door as if something had just occurred to him. "Where are the kids?"

"On the way to Chicago."

He froze in the process of peeling back both sides of her coat.

"They left *tonight?*" he asked, clearly stunned.

Colleen nodded.

"I thought they'd leave tomorrow," Eric said.

"They always leave after dinner. The kids usually fall asleep in the car. That way, they have the whole day tomorrow to goof off in the city. There's a pancake place they always have to go to for breakfast, and Marc has tickets to a basketball game tomorrow—"

He interrupted her breathless rambling.

"Why didn't you tell me?" he demanded, his manner fleetingly reminding her of how he might respond to a scattered parent who'd forgotten to tell him something crucial about his patient in the emergency room.

"I *tried* to," she said defensively, giving him a pointed

glare. "But you ran out of the house so fast, I didn't get a chance."

He released her coat like the material had burned him. "Why *are* you here?"

Not only his questions, but the blazing look in his dark eyes seemed to shine a blinding spotlight on her. She averted her gaze. Looking at him seemed to make her heart beat even more uncomfortably in her ears.

She dug deep for courage and slipped off her coat, hanging it on an antique armoire with hooks affixed alongside the mirror. She smoothed her skirt and shifted her feet, studying him through lowered lashes. "I just came to a decision, that's all."

"A decision," he said deadpan, his eyes narrowed on her, his nostrils slightly flared.

"Yes," she said with false cheerfulness. "And I really couldn't have told you earlier, because I technically just decided on my way over to your house."

"Are we talking about *the* decision…the *rational* decision?"

"That would be the one. Although…" She gulped as she met his stare. "I think we both have come to the conclusion that there isn't much rational—" she waved her finger between their bodies "—about this."

Her cheeks heated at his slow smile. He stepped toward her and leaned down. Her face was only inches away from his bare chest. His nipples were dark brown—small and erect from the chill of the outdoor temperature on his damp skin. When she inhaled, she smelled soap and felt a tingle of warmth on her lips.

His fresh, male scent and shower-steamed, heated body caused a shudder to go through her. He placed his hands on her upper arms and chafed her, mistaking her desire for cold. "Actually, I think it's the most logical choice you've ever made."

He pressed her body against his. She swore she could feel his heat emanating straight through her clothes. He kissed her, hard and sure. His tongue entered her mouth, stroking her firmly, leaving her in little doubt she was about to be claimed. He tasted like spearmint toothpaste and Eric. Colleen was thankful he had a firm grip on her, her legs grew so weak. He lifted his head a moment later and shifted his hands, stroking her sides and settling on her hips.

She gave a little squeak of alarm when he lifted her into his arms and she was airborne. She glanced up at him, embarrassed by her yelp, only to see him looking down at her, grinning.

No. Beyond grinning. He looked triumphant...like he carried a priceless treasure he'd fought hard to win.

Despite his smile, his gaze scorched as he strode down the hallway and then carried her up the stairs.

Chapter Ten

When they reached his bedroom he didn't bother to turn on a lamp, but Colleen was able to make out a few details due to the hall light flooding into the room. Two chairs with a table between them stood in a circular alcove surrounded by windows. The draperies were made of a rich, ivory colored fabric and were closed at the moment. She caught a glimpse of the bed before Eric laid her on it. It was king-size and covered in streamlined yet luxurious bedding.

Despite her anxiety, she sighed in pleasure when Eric laid her down. The duvet and pillows felt thick and soft. His singular scent filled her nose. He sat next to her on the bed, his hands still at her shoulders. His face was cast in shadow, but she saw the glint in his eyes as he looked down at her.

"You're still shivering," he murmured, rubbing her upper arms.

"I…I think it's nerves, to be honest. I haven't done this in a very long time," she said in a thin whisper.

"Are you sure about this, Colleen?"

She nodded, unable to remove her gaze from his shadowed face. "Yes. What about you?"

He laughed, low and rough, causing the back of her neck to prickle in pleasure. "Are you kidding?" He leaned down and brushed his nose against hers. She instinctively tilted her chin up, seeking out his lips with her own. A sigh caught in her throat when their mouths touched. His hand swept along the side of her sweater, lifting it. She sat forward slightly, assisting him as he whisked it over her head. She sunk back on the pillows, her long hair falling in disarray all around her.

Her entire awareness focused on the sensation of Eric's hands spread along the sides of her naked waist. He swept his palms along her ribs and back, seeming hungry to soak in the sensation of her skin against his own. The surrounding air felt cool, but Eric was warm. Hot. The contrast was delicious. Nerve endings sprung to attention wherever he touched. Pleasure swamped her awareness, leaving her a little stunned. It really had been too long for her. She'd forgotten how sublime it felt to have a man touch her.

Or had she ever known, to this degree?

Her trembling only increased when he pressed his face next to her neck, kissing her. She sunk her fingers into his damp, thick hair.

"I've waited for this for so long," he murmured next to her throat. Colleen's eyes went wide. He'd sounded a little rough...desperate. She felt a tug on her bra, and then the fabric loosened. They both moaned when his lips found hers and they kissed feverishly. Her fingertips mapped the muscles and tendons on his neck and shoulders. He was so hard, but his skin was so smooth. The contrast fascinated her. She couldn't get enough. She caught him at his neck and pressed, increasing the pressure of her kiss. His hands moved. His fingers skimmed her sensitive breasts as he pushed aside the fabric of her bra. He lightly detailed a nipple with his forefinger and a violent shudder went through her.

He sealed their kiss and lifted his head.

"Colleen?" he rasped, obviously concerned. "You're shaking. You're still cold."

"No. I mean…maybe I am a little cold. But I think it's mostly nerves. And…and…"

"What?" he whispered, stroking her face as if for reassurance.

"It feels so good," she admitted in a threadbare whisper. "I don't remember it feeling quite this…intense."

His caressing fingers stilled. It suddenly struck her that she was ruining things with all her shaking. If they just could get on with things, she knew it would eventually stop. She had faith in him. It would take all of another thirty seconds for Eric to make her forget her own name, let alone the fact that she was nervous and experiencing feelings she'd never had in her life. She leaned up, determining to resume their torrid kiss, but he halted her with a hand at her shoulder.

"Wha—?" She stopped when he stood next to the bed.

"Come on. I'm going to put you in a hot shower."

"But—"

Again, he never let her finish. He just matter-of-factly whisked her bra off her arms. Colleen's heart sunk a little when she saw he barely glanced at her breasts.

Oh, no. She really *was* ruining this.

He grabbed her hand and hustled her into the master-suite bathroom. It still felt warm and humid from Eric's earlier shower. He flipped on the light and shut the door. Colleen stood there stupidly as he turned on the shower.

"I'm sorry," she mumbled when he began to unfasten her skirt a few seconds later.

"Why? You're cold. I'm the one who should be sorry for not warming you up before I dragged you to bed."

"You hardly dragged me," Colleen muttered. She tried to brush his hands away, feeling foolish. "I can undress myself, Eric."

"I want to do it." He speared her with his gaze and Colleen dropped her hands. She'd thought him calm and collected in the past minute, but she'd thought wrong. Very wrong. His eyes told the true story. He was far, far from being unaffected by her partial nakedness.

He bent his head and resumed unfastening her skirt. It slid over her hips with his urging, falling in a pool around her ankles. He helped her step out of the fabric. She stood there wearing nothing but panties, thigh-highs and pumps. His gaze trailed over her, making her tingle wherever it touched. He placed his open hand over her belly and hip, the gesture blatantly possessive and intensely erotic. Colleen couldn't breathe.

"I can't think of what to say," he muttered, his hand stroking her waist. "You're so beautiful." His fingertips skimmed the bottom curve of one of her breasts. "So incredibly soft."

The pleasure wrought by his touch was sharp and concentrated. Her nipples pulled so tight as he caressed her, it made her hiss between a clenched jaw. He glanced into her face.

The next thing she knew, he was pulling down her panties and kneeling before her, working her thigh-highs down her legs. He held up a hand, and she grabbed it to steady herself while he removed her heels. Spikes of pleasure shot through her when he palmed her naked calf and then stroked her heel as he slipped off a shoe.

By the time he straightened, and she was naked, Colleen was trembling again from acute desire. She reached for the waistband of his sweats, but he grasped her hands, halting her.

"Get in," he said, nodding toward the shower, his voice rough. "It's nice and hot."

She went hesitantly. The steam and heat felt delicious when he slid back the glass shower door. "Eric," she called in protest when he shut the door between them.

"Just give me a second. Try to warm up," she heard him

say through the barrier of the door and the sound of the hot water pounding on the shower floor.

"I'm not that cold," she said, but she turned into the inviting heat anyway, submersing herself in the steaming, jetting water. It dismayed her a little, to think she would look like a drowned rat when Eric next saw her, but she couldn't resist the heat. She closed her eyes and put her head at the center of the spray, hastily wiping away the mascara she was quite sure was streaming down her face.

Heat and comfort coursed through her, soaking into flesh and then bone, erasing her tension.

She peered sideways, trying to discern what Eric was doing. Had he left the bathroom? The glass doors had already steamed up, obscuring her vision.

She barely had time to figure out her next move when he pulled the shower door open. Her gaze traveled over a long, muscular stretch of naked man. His male beauty and obvious desire for her left her mute. Her brain seemed to vibrate in her skull, freezing her muscles and tongue.

He stepped into the shower. The sound of the door shutting made her blink, breaking her trance.

All signs of hesitation gone, he took another step, joining her beneath the hot spray. He reached for her. The hot water, and more importantly, her desire for Eric, melted her nervousness into mist. He covered her mouth with his. She shuddered yet again at the distilled impact of his kiss combined with the delicious sensation of their naked bodies pressing close, but this was a convulsion of pure need. She felt his erection throb next to the sensitive skin of her lower belly. Her body responded of its own accord, her core clenching in desire. She gasped in protest when he lifted his head a moment later and stepped back a few inches. She clutched his shoulders, trying to draw him back, hungry for the feeling of hard male muscle pressing tight against her skin.

His smile was a little strained when he grabbed her wrist

and turned her hand, kissing her palm. "Let me look at you," he said quietly, his gaze entreating.

He looked with his eyes, but his hands traveled wherever his gaze went. He stroked her shoulders and slid his palm with rivulets of warm water along the sides of her ribs and waist. He caressed her hips and belly, and all along, Colleen was melting beneath his worshipping hands and hot stare. She, too, eagerly began to stroke him, squeezing his delightfully rounded, hard biceps in her palms, whisking her fingers across his smooth, muscular chest, running her fingertips over the discs of his flat, erect nipples.

"Don't, Colleen."

Her startled gaze leapt up to his face, his tone had been so hard. His expression turned a little contrite.

"I'm sorry," he said. He grabbed both of her wrists with warm, wet hands and moved her hands to her back. "Do you mind?" he asked.

Colleen blinked, not really sure at first what he meant. When she realized he was asking her if it was all right if he kept her hands held at her back while he touched her, heat flooded her all the way to her toes.

"That doesn't seem fair," she whispered, her gaze stuck on his sexy mouth.

He chuckled and stroked her wet neck. "You'll have your moment, trust me. Your hands are driving me nuts right now, though. I can't think. I'm about ready to lose it, I want you so bad."

Colleen glanced down the length of his aroused body and swallowed with difficulty. The admission of his vulnerability had given her strength.

"Okay," she whispered.

She watched as the hand that wasn't holding her wrists coasted through rivers of running water up her belly. He cradled a breast in his hand and shaped it to his palm.

"If you only knew how much I've fantasized about touching you," he mumbled, watching his actions with a narrow focus. "You were so beautiful in my mind, but reality is much, much better. You're exquisite," he added before he sunk his head and pressed his lips to the slope of her breast. Colleen stared into billowing steam, biting her lower lip to stifle a plea as he kissed the sensitive skin and licked away droplets of water. He took her nipple into his warm mouth, and her pleasure mounted to a piercing ache. She arched her back into him as he suckled, laving her nipple with a warm, agile tongue.

Her hip encountered his firm, heavy erection. She longed to touch him. He kept her wrists at her back, however, and she had no choice but to drown in mounting heat and pleasure. He transferred his attention to her other breast, sucking her into the heat of his mouth, lashing her nipple with his tongue, pulling on her gently until she moaned in a fever of desire.

He lifted his head and caught her mouth in a ravishing kiss. The sound of the hot water pounding on the floor drowned out her heart drumming in her ears, but her pulse throbbed madly at her throat as she kissed Eric back for all she was worth. He touched her hip, and then her pelvic bone, watching her through narrowed eyelids as his wet fingers slid over the juncture of her thighs, parting the folds of her sex. His fingers belonged to a surgeon to be sure; they were gentle, firm and astonishingly accurate.

Her eyes sprung wide as he played her most sensitive flesh.

He continued to watch her face as though fascinated by what he saw there. His finger circled and stroked until Colleen grew light-headed. He captured her whimper with his mouth, kissing her while he stroked her and pleasure surged and mounted, delicious and inescapable. The tension he wrought with his talented fingers broke.

He caught her against him as pleasure splintered through

her, eating her moans of release as though he was starved and he found them delicious.

She leaned against him, panting. She felt like she'd been turned inside out. He released her wrists and shut the water off. The cool air flowing in through the opened shower door didn't make her shiver this time.

Colleen wondered if she'd ever be cold again.

"Thank you," she murmured a moment later when Eric finished drying her off hastily with a towel. He merely swiped the same towel across his face, neck and belly before he cursed under his breath and tossed it aside. She smiled when he swept her into his arms, and suddenly they were once again in his bedroom.

"Do you make a habit of carrying women around?" she asked as he lowered her to the bed. She was so relaxed, hot and aroused, the luxurious bedding felt decadent.

"Never. You're the first. You bring out the caveman in me, apparently," he said, sounding a little grim as he searched for a condom in the bedside table. He couldn't move quickly enough for Colleen, and himself, either, from the look of his strained expression. He came down over her. His hard, lean muscles sliding against her only increased her sense of voluptuous luxury, like she was drowning in the rich, sensual world Eric had created for her. She felt as if she could melt right into the mattress…melt right into him…meld with him in a blazing, furious blast of need.

It seemed like the most natural, the most exciting thing in the world when he slid into her, fusing their flesh. She gasped at the intensity of his possession, pleasure mingling with intense, nearly untenable friction.

"Eric," she grated out between clenched teeth, because he was filling her now, overfilling her, stretching the very limits of her consciousness. "It feels—"

"Please say it feels incredible, because it *so* does," he gasped, sounding a little crazed.

"It feels incredible," she whispered.

Then he began to move, and it was as if a million pieces fell into perfect alignment. He stared down at her, his biceps bulging tight as he held himself off her. Sensations barraged her consciousness. His strokes were firm, demanding and smooth, but they caused an electric friction inside her. She was hot and melting, but she somehow needed more...more of Eric, more heat, more pressure. She was so greedy, she wanted to explode with it.

How could she have lived for so long without this divine experience?

She reached for his hips, adding her own strength to his forceful possession. He clenched his teeth and took her harder, their joining growing frantic. She met his gaze before she tipped into an abyss of pleasure.

"You're mine." His proclamation was simple, powerful... surreal.

Pleasure wracked her in waves. She felt him succumb at the very core of her being. His growl of release sounded primal...thrilling. She held him against her, feeling his shudders mingling with her own.

"Absolutely amazing," he murmured as he stroked her belly. Morning sunlight glowed behind the creamy draperies and streamed around the edges. They'd made love for a better part of the night, pausing to touch, talk and laugh in the interludes. Despite the fact that he probably had only slept a total of two hours, Eric felt energized and fantastic—better than he ever remembered feeling in his life.

He couldn't seem to keep his hands off Colleen. As a physician, the human body was his specialty. He'd learned a measure of objectivity when it came to his assessment of physical beauty. But there was something about Colleen's nudity that brought out the opposite of logic in him. She was like poetry set to flesh, all feminine curves and long, graceful limbs and beguiling stretches of smooth, silky skin. It pleased him beyond belief to find new spots where his hand fit perfectly, to seek out new patches of skin that made her breath catch and her eyes glaze with desire.

"What's absolutely amazing?" she asked after a stretched few seconds. He'd found yet another sweet spot on her side between two ribs, fracturing her attention for a moment. He leaned down to add a kiss to his tribute, and she shivered beneath his mouth. He smiled and raised his head.

"That. You're entire body is like a live wire."

Two spots of vivid color bloomed in her cheeks. "I…I'm sorry. I can't seem to help it…the shivering, I mean."

His smile faded. "Why are you apologizing? It's incredible." When she just stared at him, her blush deepening, he shook his head in disbelief. "I'm serious. What man wouldn't be thrilled having such a responsive woman in his bed? You make me feel like some kind of a god when I'm just touching you."

A small smile shaped her mouth. "You are so full of it."

He breathed a sigh of relief. She didn't entirely believe him about how intensely sexy he found her, but at least she'd relaxed enough to smile. He leaned down and kissed her, taking his time, relishing every nuance of her soft, fragrant mouth. He felt himself stir with arousal, even though they'd just finished making love minutes ago.

Her effect on him was unprecedented.

"Nicest surprise…of my life to see you standing…at my front doorstep last night," he told her between kisses a moment later. "What made you come?"

She cradled his head in her hands and sunk her fingers into his hair. His eyelids grew heavy as she massaged his scalp. Eric couldn't decide what made him happier: Colleen's magical touch or the fact that it was magic touching her. He blinked a moment later when he realized she hadn't answered his question. She was chewing on her lower lip.

Why did she look so hesitant?

"My mother said something," she began distractedly. "Something about how I was so confident in expressing my emotions…how I wasn't afraid to be honest about what I was feeling." She met his stare and gave a sheepish grin. "I realized then that not only had I not been entirely honest about how I felt about you, I had been full-out lying to myself."

He shrugged and landed another kiss on her mouth, not liking to see her looking so hesitant. "We talked about this. It isn't like there weren't barriers galore between us. Colleen?"

"Yes?" she asked, her blue-green eyes wide. She wasn't wearing a smudge of makeup and her hair was wild and uncombed. He'd discovered there were seven tiny freckles sprinkled across her nose.

She looked delectable.

"Did you make a decision to spend the night with me because you believe we can overcome those barriers?"

"I hope we can," she whispered. Her solemn expression cut at him a little. He leaned down and seized her mouth in a hot kiss. He'd rather see her beautiful face glowing with desire. She responded wholly, sweetly, melting at his touch. For a sublime moment, he made himself forget the shadow of doubt he'd seen in Colleen's expressive eyes.

Their desire spent yet again, they finally slept. Colleen awoke with her head on Eric's chest, her body wrapped in his arms. For a minute or two she lay there fully awake, soaking in the sensation of his chest rising and falling as he slept, wondering at how safe and warm she felt in his embrace.

Making love with him had been a truly eye-opening experience. Colleen had always considered herself open-minded and comfortable with the topic of sex, but Eric had taught her last night she'd never really fully explored her sexuality. Thanks to him, she'd just begun to tap into the depths of her sensual nature, and for that she'd be forever thankful. She couldn't recall ever feeling so alive, so feminine…so wonderful.

When she finally focused on the clock on the bedside table, her eyes widened in disbelief. She hadn't slept until noon since she was a carefree teenager. Of course, then she hadn't possessed the adult excuse of being kept awake all night by a virile, demanding man. She eased out of Eric's arms, trying not to wake him. He roused slightly, his forehead crinkling and his mouth flattening, like he was dissatisfied with something and was about to take someone to task in his dreams. Colleen smiled, recalling how at one time, she would have interpreted that exact expression as arrogance.

Today, she decided that expression was entirely endearing.

She wasn't thrilled about putting on her clothes from last night, but what other choice did she have? She detangled her hair with effort. Eric still slept as she crept downstairs, eager to call her children. Brendan and Jenny were having too good of a time, however, to spend much time on the phone with her. After she hung up, Colleen found herself longing for clean clothes. Could she run to her house and retrieve some before Eric woke? She didn't want to disturb his sleep if she didn't have to.

She was putting on her coat in the foyer when something caught her attention. Eric strode down the hallway. Her eyes went wide. He wore a pair of jeans and a scowl.

"Where are you going?" he demanded. "You're not leaving."

She smiled. The last part hadn't been a question, but a proclamation. He seemed a little distraught and that pleased her, although she couldn't really believe for two seconds he was seriously upset. Surely a man like him was used to a woman scurrying away in the morning after a night of passion spent in his bed, even if the odds were Eric was the one sneaking out of bed and dashing out the door while the woman still slept. In fact, it had occurred to her that if she left his house, he might think it was very odd for her to return, so his reaction reassured and warmed her.

He looked incredibly sexy standing there, bare-chested and hair mussed. He must have dressed in a hurry before he came downstairs, because the top two buttons of his jeans were still unfastened. The triangle of bare skin exposed above the partially opened fly was paler than his abdomen.

She yanked her gaze to his face.

"I didn't want to wake you. I wanted to shower, but I didn't have anything clean to put on. I was thinking about running home to get a few things."

He stepped toward her and slid her coat off her shoulders. "The easiest solution to that problem would be for you to stay naked all weekend," he said in a sultry tone.

"Not even you could have that much energy." She glanced up as he took her coat and noticed his small smile. "All right," she conceded. "I admit that you just might."

"Only when truly inspired," he said gruffly, reaching for her. He kissed her, and she looped her arms around his waist. "I did not like waking up and finding you gone."

"Hmm, yes, you've made that clear. But I need clothes."

He growled softly and kissed her again. "I'll take you to your house and you can get what you need for the rest of the weekend." He deepened their kiss. Colleen went up on her tiptoes, flushing with heat. "But right now, let's go back to bed," he mumbled next to her lips a moment later.

"No," Colleen scolded, even though she was sorely tempted. "It's the afternoon, and I haven't even had my morning coffee yet."

He lifted his head. How could she have ever hated his brooding scowls? She resisted an urge to pull him down again for another kiss. At this point, she knew full well how delicious even his frowns tasted on her hungry lips.

"Okay," he conceded ungraciously. "I suppose I'll have to feed you, too."

"You really are a gentleman."

He smiled, his dark eyes gleaming. "A gentleman wouldn't have taken you to bed without taking you on at least one official date."

"Dinner last night didn't count?" she murmured.

He shook his head with mock sadness before he kissed her nose. "Nope. I have some karma to make up in the dating department. Give me fifteen minutes to get ready. Afterward, I'll make up for my callousness by giving you a day you'll never forget. I'll do my best, anyway."

"Your best is pretty damn amazing so far."

His eyes widened and then smoldered at her honesty. "Are you sure you don't want to—"

She laughed and gave him a gentle shove. "*No.* Get going. I can't wait to see what you come up with to balance your dating karma. Not that I'm putting any pressure on you or anything."

He grinned and backed out of the foyer, keeping his eyes on her the whole time. "I'm a surgeon, remember? I thrive on pressure."

She rolled her eyes.

"Fifteen minutes," he promised.

"I'm timing you."

He charged for the stairs.

Colleen caught a glimpse of herself in the armoire mirror. She blinked. Her cheeks were flushed and she was grinning like an idiot. It took her a moment to recognize her own face transformed by pure happiness.

Oh, no. Something squirmed in her stomach.

Surely it was a mistake for her to allow herself to be this happy.

Don't think about that. Just try and live in the moment for once. Don't you deserve a nice, carefree weekend?

Colleen waited, wondering if the anxiety monster in her belly would rear to life again. When it remained silent, she sighed with relief. Her anticipation for spending time with Eric was free to build. Nervousness segued to pure excitement.

Chapter Eleven

After Eric took her to her house for a quick shower and change of clothing, they went to refuel at the Tap and Grill. The Tap was known for selling breakfast at all hours, so they filled up on omelets, wheat toast, coffee and orange juice, both of them unabashedly ravenous after their night of love-making. They talked almost nonstop. Eric kept her in stitches, telling her about several funny odd jobs he'd held in college and medical school, including a job in a toothpaste factory and another dusting dinosaur bones at the Detroit Science Center. At one point, he noticed her distracted expression.

"What's wrong?" he asked.

Colleen shook her head and took a sip of coffee. "All those jobs you worked…" She faded off hesitantly. She studied the remains of her toast, suddenly unable to meet his gaze. "Wasn't there sufficient money from the lawsuit? I mean… it was quite a lot, wasn't it? I…I would have thought—"

He silenced her increasingly nervous ramblings by placing his hand on top of hers. She met his stare.

"You know how expensive college and medical school are, let alone food, board and other living expenses. Natalie was only eleven when the crash happened. I needed to be careful with finances. I had her to support. I didn't want to screw up and find out she didn't have all the resources she needed to go to college. So I supplemented with odd jobs."

"I'm sorry you had to grow up so young, Eric."

"I thought you said last night that you realized you can't apologize for your dad's actions."

"I did," she said quietly. "I'm not apologizing for Dad. I'm just sorry things were so rough for you."

He squeezed her hand, and she looked up. "I turned out okay."

"Yeah. You did," she whispered feelingly.

Eric wouldn't tell her where he planned to take her after they ate, so Colleen was a little taken aback when he pulled his car into Sutter Park's outdoor ice rink.

"Ice-skating?" she asked incredulously. "But I can't skate."

"Come on," he encouraged. "It'll be fun. Look, they have all the Christmas decorations up."

Colleen was extremely doubtful about the venture. The Kavanaughs were water lovers, one and all, but she didn't care for the frozen variety. Even she had to admit the atmosphere at the outdoor rink was festive, though. The big Christmas tree they always put up in the park twinkled in the distance. Red and green lights had been strung around the low brick wall enclosing the rink. Kids shouted and zoomed around the ice. Christmas carols played over the loudspeaker. Even the weather cooperated with the holiday atmosphere. Fat snowflakes began to fall as they headed for the ice.

Colleen tottered in her rented skates, Eric's hold on her arm the only thing keeping her from doing a face-plant.

"Bend your knees more," Eric encouraged. Colleen grimaced. He was holding her hands and skating backward with effortless ease. It was clear that his years of playing hockey had turned him into an excellent skater. He made skating backward look as easy as breathing. His movements were graceful, but not elegant like a figure skater's. He was brawny strength set into effortless motion. Colleen had a hard time focusing on her own awkward movements; she was so busy admiring him.

She wavered and almost fell before Eric steadied her. "The blade is too skinny," she protested, frowning at the six-year-olds who flew past her like bullets. "I have no balance whatsoever."

Eric suspected she hadn't tied her skates tight enough and pulled her over to a bench, Colleen's ankles wiggling like two pieces of cooked spaghetti the whole time. He knelt before her and efficiently relaced and retied her skates. "Better?" he asked a moment later, wrapping both her calves in his gloved hands.

"We'll see," she said, warmed by his gaze and massaging palms.

She noticed him grinning a few minutes later.

"Now you're getting it," he said in a complimentary tone, referring to her skating.

Colleen thought he might be right. She was starting to learn the required motion to propel herself forward while maintaining a tricky balance. Eric casually turned directions and dropped one of her hands, skating next to her instead of in front.

"Show-off," she muttered, grinning.

She ended up having a ball. It was refreshing, good exercise, and Eric was excellent company. They skated and drank hot chocolate and skated again. For the first hour or so, the temperature hovered around the freezing point and there was little wind, making her unaware of the cold. Besides, Eric kept her warm with his flashing grins and effortless athletic grace.

At one point, however, Eric yanked gently on her hand and

brought her to a halt, pulling her to the side, away from the zooming skaters. He brushed several snowflakes out of her unbound hair and off her cheeks. He frowned when a tremor went through her.

"You're shaking again," he murmured. "It's getting colder. We should go."

"Maybe you're right," she said a little regretfully. "I really *am* shivering from the cold this time."

His eyebrows arched at that, as if he'd recalled what else made her tremble. He leaned down and covered her mouth was his. His kiss made her wonder if he'd transformed the snowflakes on her lips from ice straight to steam.

After they left the skating rink, they went to a movie at the local theatre. It was beyond nice to rest her cheek on Eric's chest while his arm encircled her, eating popcorn and soaking up his heat. The movie was forgettable.

The moment wasn't.

"You made a lot of progress on your dating karma," she murmured later as they drove back to his house. Eric had taken her out for an intimate, delicious dinner at a local seafood restaurant. Colleen was feeling drowsy and content.

"Still work to be done, though?" he asked, taking her hand in his. "Don't worry. I've got plenty more where that came from."

She chuckled and gazed out the window lazily. "I don't know how much more courting you're going to get in. A big storm is predicted over the weekend."

"All the better. Indoor activities are my specialty."

Colleen grinned wryly, but she didn't refute him. He had a point.

When they returned to his house, she made some tea while Eric built a fire. While they were separated, she experienced an urge to clarify his intentions about getting involved with her. She quashed the idea almost as soon as she had it. She despised the needy female stereotype. *Just what is it, exactly, that we're doing here?*

Just thinking about the predictable phrase featured in dozens of chick flicks and romantic comedies made her cringe. Why did men have to be the only ones who were supremely comfortable not questioning motives at the beginning of relationships and just taking things as they came?

No, she assured herself. She would not turn into a simpering idiot just because she liked a man. She'd take this one step at a time, like Eric was doing. Just because she was a novice in the world of sex and dating didn't mean she was naive. Experience and knowledge were two different things, and she'd racked up years of knowledge being a professional counselor.

"Do you want to work on *Lucy* tomorrow?" she asked him once she'd brought out the tea and they were sipping it on the couch before the fire.

"Sure, if you do."

"The wedding is only two weeks away. I can't believe it. I still haven't gotten them a wedding present," she murmured, setting her cup on the coffee table. She leaned back and snuggled against Eric's side. He put his arm around her. The heat from the fire warmed her cheeks.

"We'll say *Lucy* is from all of us."

Colleen lifted her head, blushing. "No...I didn't mean anything like that—"

"I know you didn't," he said. "Still, it only seems right. You, the kids and your mother have worked on her. Brendan asked me point-blank if he could help restoring *Lucy*. That takes a serious time commitment for someone his age. He's a great kid. So's Jenny."

She shook her head in amazement. He quirked one eyebrow at her.

"What?" he asked, grinning.

"I can't believe I ever thought you were arrogant."

His grin faded. He leaned forward and deposited his cup on the coffee table. He put out his arms, reaching for her. "Come here," he said gruffly.

Colleen went without hesitation. Nothing in the world sounded so appealing to her at that moment as the idea of sitting in his lap and having his arms surround her. And it *was* nice, she acknowledged a second later when she settled on his thighs, facing him, her knees bent at her side and her hands around his neck.

Not as nice as when she leaned forward and kissed him with the force of all the emotions she had brewing in her chest. Not as nice as when Eric returned the kiss with undisguised fervor and admirable skill.

"I've been waiting to do that since I woke up this morning," she told him a while later, her damp lips brushing against his as she spoke.

"I've been waiting for you to do that for half my life."

She laughed. He delighted her. She kissed him again. He opened his hands along her hips and buttocks, scooting her forward on his thighs. Their embrace was very similar to that night after the engagement party on her couch. Intimate. Heated.

It was drastically different, too. Tonight, Colleen's desire had been liberated.

She ran her fingers through his hair, and then tilted his head, turning hers at an angle to deepen their kiss. He groaned, and she transferred her mouth to his throat, relishing the vibrations of his desire on her lips. She ran her fingers fleetly down his chest and belly, unbuttoning his outer shirt. Beneath it, he wore a Detroit Red Wings T-shirt. He seemed all too eager to assist her struggle in getting him out of it, post haste.

She kissed his bare chest a moment later, submerging herself in the sensation of him. She gave herself full permission to forget everything but the gorgeous, delicious male she currently sampled with lips, tongue and teeth. He hissed when she bit gently at a hard, rounded shoulder muscle. He began to lift up her sweater, but she stopped him.

"Remember last night?" she asked breathlessly. "When you said I'd have my moment to touch you? Now's the moment."

His nostrils flared slightly. She pressed a kiss just below his right nipple and glanced up at him. She thought his stare would burn her when she placed her lips directly over the nipple. He was still watching her, his face rigid and his eyes blazing, when she scooted back on his thighs and tested the texture of his taut abdomen with her lips. His muscles leapt at her touch, sending a thrill through her. Her hair fell forward, swishing across his stomach.

He hissed like she'd scalded him.

He put his hands on her shoulders and pulled her up to him. He consumed her with a kiss so hot, it melted her all the way from her core to her toes and the roots of the hair on her head. He started to undress her. Colleen didn't protest this time. It felt too amazing, and besides, if she gave him enough practice, maybe he'd get used to the idea of her being the one to ravish him once in a while. A girl could always hope, anyway.

And it *was* a nice, long weekend…

The next day they lingered in bed until late morning. Eric had pulled back the draperies on the window that faced Lake Michigan. They held each other and watched the heavy snowfall.

"Did you ever consider becoming anything besides a doctor?" Colleen mused during one of their many murmured conversations. She lay on her side, facing the snowy window. Eric's long body traced hers from behind. She dreamily was stroking his forearm, which surrounded her belly.

"Sure. I wanted to be a hockey player. What kid doesn't

dream of being a professional athlete? My mom wasn't too thrilled about the idea." He chuckled and nuzzled her neck. She felt his smile pressed against her skin when a shiver coursed through her.

"Was it your mother who wanted you to be a doctor?"

"Yes. Luckily, I decided the same thing before she died. The winter that I was seventeen, I got a bad knee injury during the high-school playoffs. I was out of commission. Thought my life was over. My mom made a comfortable life for Natalie and me, but she worked her hands to the bone to do it. She couldn't afford insurance. She'd religiously save money every month for Natalie's and my medical care. When I started working, she made me do the same thing.

"My knee was really screwed up after the playoffs, and the doctors said I needed surgery. We didn't have the money to pay for it. I took the news hard…acted like a real ass," he said bluntly.

Colleen turned in his arms. "What do you mean?"

"I thought hockey was my whole world. My golden ticket. I sulked a lot when my mother told me we couldn't afford the surgery."

"That's not too surprising," Colleen murmured. "Not if hockey meant so much to you, and you were so talented at it."

He shrugged. "I made such a big deal about it, my mom did something she'd never considered before. She applied to get state medical aid."

Colleen studied the angry slant of his mouth and averted gaze. It obviously still bothered him that his mother had done such a thing for him.

"She was your mother, Eric," Colleen said softly. "She didn't apply for the aid because you were being a sulky teenager. She did it because she would have done whatever was necessary to get you the care you needed."

"You think so?" he asked levelly.

She touched his shoulder. "I know so. I'm a single mother, just like your mother was. I'd do the same for Brendan and Jenny in a second if I had no other choice," she whispered feelingly.

His gaze flickered over her face before he brushed his finger over her jaw. "Maybe you're right. Anyway, it ended up being the best thing that ever happened to me. My orthopedic surgeon's name was Mac Harkman. Harkman loved what he did, and he managed to pass his enthusiasm on to me. When he found out I was a natural in math and science, he sort of took me under his wing. He joined league with my mom in encouraging me to go to medical school. Changed my life, I guess you could say."

Colleen smiled. "And we're all luckier for it, Brendan and I included," she murmured before she kissed him. He groaned and came down over her, pressing her back into the mattress.

The snow continued to fall outside the window, thick and silent, but they were too absorbed in one another for the next half hour to notice.

They finally got up, showered and made a breakfast of whole-wheat toast, scrambled eggs and fruit. After Colleen had called Brendan and Jenny, hearing their enthusiastic report of the good time they were having in Chicago, they began working on *Lucy*. By the time they called it quits at around nightfall, *Lucy* looked glossy and smart with her second coat of varnish.

Eric looked out a window in the kitchen. "The snow is getting thick on the ground. I'll get out the snowblower in the morning. It's a good thing we took your car back to your house, though. It might have gotten stuck. I'll be able to take you home in the SUV tomorrow."

Her eyes went wide when he abruptly turned around, an odd, intense expression on his handsome face, and stalked over to her. She'd been in the process of getting some tea bags out of the cupboard, but she dropped the box when she noticed his determination. She yelped in amazement when he lifted her and set her on the counter before him.

"What are you doing?" She laughed when he pressed his mouth to her neck and started kissing her hungrily, his hands busily unbuttoning her shirt.

"I just realized I don't want to take you home. How would you feel about me kidnapping you indefinitely?" he growled softly before he slipped his hand between the folds of her shirt and over her left breast.

Her heart hitched beneath his palm, but then he seized her mouth and she forgot everything but his scent, his texture, his heat. How could a man who had once claimed to be the champion of rational thought have the capability to erase it so completely from her brain?

Eric drifted off to sleep, but Colleen wasn't tired. She was feeling pensive and a little heartsore. Eric's lovemaking had been wild, delicious and intense. Did he recognize that their time together was drawing to a close? All the what-ifs she'd been shoving into the periphery of her brain while she luxuriated in her time with Eric started to crowd to the forefront once again.

She got up, dressed in a pair of yoga pants and a sweatshirt, and wandered downstairs. She checked her cell phone for messages and saw Mari had called. Worried something was wrong with the kids, she called her back. Mari hadn't been calling about the kids, however. Instead, she wanted to get all the details about what was happening between her and Eric. Since Colleen was feeling especially vulnerable on that particular topic, she managed to make light of Mari's inquiries and cut the conversation short.

After she'd hung up with Mari, she noticed her sister, Deidre, had called. She immediately returned the call.

"Deidre? Is everything all right?"

It turned out that everything was not all right. Death hovered close in Lincoln DuBois's Lake Tahoe mansion tonight. It broke Colleen's heart to hear her usually fearless, indomitable sister sounding so fragile and lost.

"The kids are with Marc and Mari this weekend," Colleen said after they'd talked awhile, her mind spinning into crisis mode. "As soon as we get off the phone, I'll call and get a plane ticket to Reno."

"No, that's okay. Linc… Well, he's not gone yet," Deidre murmured in her characteristic low, smoky voice.

"You can't go through this alone, Deidre," she said, looking nervously out Eric's front window, her thoughts coming rapidly. Would the snow prevent her from catching a flight out of Detroit? Maybe the conditions at Chicago's airports would be better.

"I'm not alone. Linc's doctor and two hospice nurses are here…along with Nick Malone."

"You mean Lincoln's Chief Executive Officer? I thought he'd gone to the San Francisco offices and left you in peace," Colleen said, concerned. She'd gotten the distinct impression from Deidre that her biological father's right-hand man was more than just a business acquaintance: he was like an adopted son. Malone was highly suspicious of Deidre's sudden appearance and Linc's official proclamation that she was his daughter. Colleen had always looked up to and admired her older sister. A fortune hunter was the last thing Deidre was, but apparently Nick Malone didn't believe that. Colleen had to wonder if he wasn't so irritated by Deidre's sudden appearance because he was worried she'd steal some portion of the pie he'd been counting on as his own from Lincoln DuBois's inheritance.

"He did leave for a while, but he's back," Deidre said, her flat tone becoming a little more animated. "He's one of the coldest, most paranoid people I've ever met, but I can't fault him for being here. Linc isn't doing well, and Malone is concerned. I may not like him, but there's no doubt that Lincoln cares about him." She sighed. "You should have seen how he lit up when Nick came into the room."

It pained Colleen to consider everything her sister had gone through in the past few months. "Deidre, I refuse to leave you there without any family to support you, especially if Nick Malone is giving you a hard time."

"I can handle Malone," she stated, her mellifluous voice going grim. Suddenly, Colleen had a clear vision of her sister in her mind's eye, the determination stiffening her delicate features, the steely expression that entered her large, grayish blue eyes just before she tried a risky new ski jump or new dive. Deidre was a daredevil, a championship diver, trick-skier and a decorated army nurse, but Colleen couldn't help but feel that her fearlessness could only get her so far during this difficult trial. "Just promise you'll come to Tahoe if… when…Linc—"

"I will," Colleen said firmly when Deidre wavered. "The second you call. And after everything is settled, I really want you to consider coming back to Harbor Town with me."

"I can't even go that far in my mind, right now. I'm already feeling overwhelmed with the fact that I'm losing Linc when I just found him. He's the second father Mom stole from me," Deidre whispered.

Her heart squeezed in her chest when she heard a muffled sob through the receiver.

Colleen wanted to weep, too. She loved Deidre. She loved her mother, even though she knew Brigit had made a terrible mistake in lying about Deidre's paternity. She wanted to knit things back together between mother and daughter, and knowing that it was beyond her control hurt. It hurt a lot.

It was all such a mess.

She stayed on the phone a while longer, trying her best to bring Deidre comfort. When she did eventually hang up, she sat curled up in the corner of Eric's couch, feeling lost. She wasn't sure how long she sat there, feeling miserable. The next thing she knew, Eric was coming down next to her and his arms were surrounding her.

She lost control at his touch. For some reason, his compassionate, strong embrace made the dam break. She sobbed with emotion. She'd held so much inside of her since that night last summer when she'd heard her mother's confession about her affair with Lincoln DuBois and her subsequent pregnancy with his child—Deidre. It bewildered her, this upsurge of emotion. Sadness, worry, hurt and anger swelled and spilled to the surface. Eric didn't say anything but just held her and made soothing noises. When her storm began to recede, however, Colleen knew she had to offer some kind of explanation. He stood to get her a box of tissues.

"I'm sorry. Here I go again. You really must think I'm a basket case," she mumbled, wiping off her cheeks with the tissue he offered her.

"I don't think that at all." He sat down next to her again on the couch and put his arms around her. He'd pulled on a clean T-shirt and jeans before he came downstairs. The clean cotton smelled good when she pressed her cheek against it. He stroked her back. "Who were you talking to? Are the kids okay?"

Colleen realized he'd noticed her cell phone sitting on the couch cushion next to her. "I was talking to my sister, Deidre," she whispered.

"Is she okay?" he asked, concerned.

"She's fine. It's…Lincoln DuBois. He's dying."

"The family friend? The one she's visiting in Lake Tahoe? Natalie told me something about it. Isn't he *the* DuBois of DuBois Enterprises?"

Colleen swallowed thickly. She'd shared so much with him in the past few days. Somehow, lying to him given their new closeness felt wrong. Very wrong. She lifted her head and met his stare.

"Yes. Lincoln DuBois isn't just an old friend of my mother's," she whispered. "He's Deidre's biological father. That's what Liam and Natalie discovered last summer, when they investigated the reason Derry was so upset on the night of the crash. My father had encountered some medical information about Deidre that made him suspect she couldn't be his biological daughter. He confronted my mother about it on the afternoon of the accident, and my mother had admitted the truth about her affair with DuBois and her suspicion that Deidre was his child. That's why my father got so drunk that night...the night he killed your mother and injured Natalie."

Eric's stroking hand stilled on her back. His expression looked flat...incredulous. The sound of the furnace turning on interrupted the thick silence.

"Deidre is out there in Tahoe with none of us there. She just told me DuBois is near death. She's losing another father, just when she got to know him, and she's so angry at my mom...and there's *nothing* I can do." She broke at the last, a fresh convulsion of grief tearing through her. Eric tightened his hold on her while she wept.

"I thought about telling you before," Colleen said, lifting her head off his chest and straining to compose herself.

"Why didn't you?" he asked.

She shrugged. "Embarrassment?" More tears spilled down her cheeks, and she wiped them away impatiently. "I used to think my parents were the perfect couple, but in the background, in secret, all this drama was taking place, and it's so...*tawdry,*" she spit out. "It's bad enough that the crash happened...that you lost your mother, and Mari lost her parents, and Natalie went through all that pain. But the reason behind it is so shameful."

Her gaze flickered over him. He looked sober as a judge. He inhaled slowly, and she found herself on pins and needles, wondering what he would say. He placed his hands on her jaw, tilting her face so she was forced to meet his stare.

"I understand why you didn't want to tell me at first."

"You do?"

"You must be torn up by this. Of course you're not going to be shouting it out to every stranger who walks by. I imagine it'll take a while for you and your family to sort all this out. But believe this," he said firmly. "You have nothing, *nothing* to be ashamed of. You had as much control over your parents' actions as I do."

"I know," she said honestly. "But that's how it is with family. You share the burden of the guilt. It's hard to just let it go. It's not that easy, especially when I see how their mistakes have affected people in the here and now…people like you, and Natalie and Deidre. How can an act of infidelity have such far-reaching consequences?"

He leaned down and kissed her lips tenderly. "You aren't the responsible one. You can't control other people's fates, Colleen. I understand that the truth can be sad, and that it can hurt, but it's not in your power to change it." She looked into his eyes and saw his compassion, but also just a hint of a challenge. "Remember how I said a while back that you and I are a lot alike?"

She nodded.

"I know it's hard for you relinquish control in a situation like this, to admit that you can't be the one to make everything better. That's why you're so good at your job, because you don't give up on your patients. You keep fighting. Just like I do for mine. But sometimes, you have to be able to admit that you can't control things. People we care about are going to get hurt, and they're going to make mistakes. Sometimes people die, too," he whispered hoarsely. "And you have to be able to let go, to admit you can't play God and control their destiny."

She sobbed quietly. He was one hundred percent right. She was the nurturer of the family, the one who always smoothed things over and strove for harmony. At work, she hated admitting defeat with her patients and rarely did. Eric was right about something else. He really did understand her because they were similar in that way; they'd fought similar internal battles with accepting when things were beyond their control.

He made a hushing sound and kissed the tears from her cheeks.

"Will you do something for me?" he murmured.

"Yes."

"Let go of it, Colleen. I know you can't stop worrying about people. I know you can't stop caring. But please…let go of the responsibility. Let go of the shame." His face pinched slightly, as if he was pained. "I can't stand to think of you holding on to it."

"I'll try," she said earnestly. "I will."

She leaned into him, suddenly needy for his heat. She sought out his mouth with her lips. While their mouths still clung in a kiss, he shifted her into his lap. A moment later, when he stood with her in his arms, they didn't speak. There was no need to talk. Their gazes said it all.

He carried her upstairs, laid her on his unmade bed and began to undress her. Colleen let him, even though she felt more naked and exposed than she ever had in her life.

But more beautiful, as well, she admitted, taking in Eric's gaze as it trailed down over her naked body.

He stripped and came down next to her on the bed. He kissed her everywhere, sanctifying her with his touch, cleansing her with the fires of desire. When his head settled between her thighs, she accepted his most intimate kiss, opening herself to him. She felt vulnerable, but she felt whole, as well. His lips and tongue worshipped her with an avid, concise prayer. It stole her breath, the pleasure he brought her. She cried out as bliss flooded her, fierce and distilled.

He swallowed her whimpers with his kiss, their essences mingling. His possession was forceful and total, leaving her in little doubt that he'd been suffering the tortures of his own need while he'd brought her such sweet pleasure. He whispered in her ear roughly as their passion peaked, and she felt herself once again hovering on the precipice of climax.

"That's right. Let go. Give yourself to me."

She'd been so afraid of fully exploring the boundaries of her passion, afraid of what it would be like to fall from the lofty heights of ecstasy to the dark abyss of loss and betrayal. But in that moment, Colleen took a chance. She let go and leaped.

Eric was right there with her, holding her, fusing with her, a full partner, sharing in the sensual storm.

Chapter Twelve

The next morning the snowstorm had stopped. They worked together to clear Eric's driveway. She'd talked to Marc, and he'd said to expect him and the kids at around two o'clock that afternoon.

Her weekend with Eric had been electric and vivid. All of her senses were peaked and sharp, as though she'd undergone a sensual awakening. But as she walked out the front door with Eric, she suddenly felt as flat and gray as the early December sky. It was time to return to her work and routine. She had no idea what the future would look like for her and Eric.

They went to Sultan's for breakfast, and Colleen couldn't help but be struck by the difference between this meal with Eric and their first at the restaurant a few weeks ago. They both sipped their coffee and shared the Sunday paper, their hands clasped on the tabletop. Every once in a while, she'd glance up and catch Eric watching her. What was he thinking as he studied her so soberly? She hated the fact that while they appeared to be the very image of a content, sensually connected couple, her doubtful thoughts and annoying questions about where the relationship was going started to harp at her again.

An hour later, Eric pulled into her driveway. He was due at the hospital within the hour in order to carry out a monthly mandatory shift in the emergency room. Neither of them spoke as he put the SUV in Park.

"Thank you," she said quietly. "It was a wonderful weekend."

"You hardly need to thank me, when I enjoyed it so much."

Colleen cleared her throat. Was it her imagination, or had the silence just become awkward…charged? All her doubts flooded to the surface. She opened her mouth, unable to stop herself from voicing a question about how he felt about the relationship on a go-forward basis. He spoke before she could, however.

"Colleen…you've been so honest with me over the weekend," he began. "I've appreciated that. I feel like I owe you a truth in return."

Her heart fluttered in her chest. "What?" His seriousness had set an alarm bell going off in her head.

"It's just…" He paused and stared out the front window, seeming uncertain how to phrase his words. "When I operated on Brendan, and then when Liam and Natalie announced they were getting married, I realized there was a certain opportunity available to me that hadn't been there before."

"Opportunity?"

His flickering gaze bounced off her face. "Yeah. I told you earlier this week that I've always been attracted to you. But because of our history, you'd put a barrier the size of the Great Wall of China between us. It was damn near impossible for me to get anywhere near you. Every time I tried to…"

"Get me into bed?" she finished for him numbly when he faded off. His dark-eyed gaze met hers.

"I'm not going to deny that I always wanted you. Every time I tried to get near you though, you erected another layer on your wall. You blocked me at every turn."

"So you used my son and the wedding to get what you wanted," she clarified. She couldn't believe she sounded so calm.

"Well...yeah, but I wasn't dishonest about anything. I think I made it pretty clear how interested I was."

"So why the need to confess?"

He blinked at her quiet question. Her heartbeat now roared in her ears.

"You always came off as so strong...so...impenetrable, like nothing could get to you. After last night," he said gruffly, "I realized that was an illusion, though. I realized how hard it must have been for you to start up with me when you had so many doubts about a relationship since Darin died...and because of your discovery about what happened with your mom's infidelity. It made me feel guilty."

"Why?" Colleen breathed out, dreading his answer.

"Because when I started this thing, I considered it...I considered *you*...as sort of a...challenge," he said abruptly. He averted his gaze when she just stared at him. "I'd always wanted you, and I never could think of a way to make it happen."

"A challenge," she muttered through lips that had suddenly gone numb. Her hands and feet began to tingle uncomfortably. She couldn't believe this was happening. She couldn't believe he was saying these things when she'd taken such a risk in letting down her guard. "Oh my God," she whispered.

"What?" he asked, looking over at her sharply.

"You called me a princess that day on Sunset Beach. You made it seem like you always considered me a...a...stuck-up witch. Is that the challenge you wanted?" she asked incredulously. "To put me in my place once and for all? Bed the bitch and show her who was really boss?"

It was like the past few months had never occurred. They might have been standing alone on Sunset Beach all over again, Colleen vibrating with anger and angst over the fact that Eric Reyes had trumped her yet again. The silence rang in her ears. He looked stricken.

"No! Of course not. Don't jump to ridiculous conclusions."

"Ridiculous? You're the one who just told me you maneuvered the circumstances…took advantage of me in order to get me into bed."

"I was trying to be honest and admit my intentions in the beginning. There's nothing criminal about me wanting you, Colleen."

"You manipulated me," she said in a low, shaking voice. Her whole body seemed to throb in pain. "You engineered all that stuff about us working together to convince Natalie and Liam they were being so impulsive and irrational about falling so fast for each other. The whole time you were probably sitting back and laughing over the fact that I was falling in love with you just as hard, just as rashly…just as stupidly."

His furious expression softened. "You were falling in love with me?"

Her eyes went wide. She couldn't believe she'd just said that. Talk about letting down her armor at the moment when the blows were raining down the hardest. Frustration overwhelmed her. It was so unfair, how he always managed to get under her skin…weaken her.

"Don't worry," she grated out. "I've come to my senses. Thanks for helping me to see things again in such a rational light, Reyes."

"Colleen, wait," he ordered, grabbing her hand, trying to halt her exit. "You're completely misinterpreting what I'm trying to say. Let me finish, for God's sake—"

But she'd had enough. Enough of this hurt, enough of this risk…enough of her immense stupidity and naïveté for allowing herself to fall hopelessly in love with Eric Reyes.

He'd done it all because she'd been a challenge. He'd dared himself to do the impossible…to melt the ice princess. Well, he'd succeeded.

She shook off his hold, grabbed her bag and stumbled out of the SUV. The frigid outdoor air struck her face like a much-needed slap of reality.

Three days later, Colleen found herself knocking on the front door of the most grand and elegant mansion she'd ever seen. Crisp, cool alpine air, tall, majestic pine trees and snow-capped High Sierra Mountains surrounded her. Her trip to Reno and then Lake Tahoe had started last night, when Deidre had called with the sad news that her newly found father, Lincoln DuBois, had died. Colleen had prepared with a plan for the circumstances. She had plenty of vacation time she could take at work. She'd told her sister she'd be in Lake Tahoe by the next afternoon.

It had done her good to be able to focus on something and someone other than herself. She still felt rattled by what had happened with Eric over the weekend, wounded by the re-alization of how her life had changed in such a short period of time. She'd fallen in love without ever giving herself per-mission to do so, and it was perhaps that realization that had left her reeling most of all.

The trip to be with Deidre gave her something solid to focus on; something tangible and worthwhile, unlike her mis-guided love affair with Eric.

She'd been glad to have the kids home and to return to her normal schedule. Unfortunately, Eric had called her on the same evening he'd dropped her off. She hadn't answered it, since it was impossible to ignore the anger, hurt and bewil-derment she was feeling at what had occurred between them.

The next day, she was again forced to face the music when Brendan reminded her on the way to school that they were all going to be working on *Lucy* that evening. Since Colleen had granted permission for it last week, she couldn't easily back out on her promise without calling attention to the fact that her and Eric's relationship had altered over the weekend. So instead of letting the kids down, she called her mother and left a message explaining she'd have to work late that evening. She'd added that her mother should check with Eric about the plans, just to make sure he was still interested in having them. She'd stayed late at The Family Center, working on paperwork, feeling lonely and heartsore the whole time.

She'd continued to avoid Eric's phone calls, but knew she'd have to face seeing him on Wednesday, when he came for his weekly volunteer hours at The Family Center. She'd been both relieved and disappointed that Lincoln DuBois's death and her subsequent trip to Lake Tahoe had prevented her from ever seeing him at work.

Now two thousand miles separated her and Eric. Before she could experience a stab of pain over that thought, the heavy front door swung open and she was staring at her sister standing in the opening, wearing jeans and a tight dark blue T-shirt.

They say that you always admire what you don't have when it comes to looks, and for Colleen that was especially true about how she felt about Deidre. Only their coloring was similar. Colleen was taller and more curvy than her sister. She'd always envied Deidre's coltish long legs, slim hips and toned, shapely figure. Deidre looked even more slender than she'd been the last time Colleen had seen her in Chicago, on a mutual visit with Marc and Liam. Her recent anguish had seemed to hollow out her cheeks and make her exceptional bluish gray eyes look even larger and more striking than usual.

They flew into each other's arms.

"Oh my God, I'm so happy to see you. You couldn't have come at a better time. Better time for me that is," Deidre said, leaning back and inspecting her sister. "I know it couldn't have been easy for you to pick up and leave, given the kids and work…and Eric," Deidre finished softly.

Something about seeing Deidre after such a long absence and hearing her say Eric's name caused emotion to swell in Colleen's chest. She and Deidre had spoken frequently on the phone in the past week. Colleen had eventually broken down and spilled the story to Deidre's sympathetic ear.

She ruffled Deidre's silky, glossy blond hair. The short style emphasized both Deidre's strong, unique character and her delicate features to perfection. She didn't wear a smudge of makeup. Deidre had been gifted with move-star-quality beauty, but as always, she seemed sublimely unaware of it. It'd been so hard to be separated from her sister by half the planet for so long. Colleen vowed then and there to do whatever she could to convince Deidre to come back to Michigan with her.

"I wouldn't be anyplace in the world right now but by your side," Colleen assured, glancing around her. In the distance, she glimpsed a spectacular great room and enormous picture window overlooking a stunning view of a sapphire-blue Lake Tahoe. "You'd do the same for me in similar circumstances. A man can't come between sisters."

She was glad to see the mischievous sparkle return to Deidre's eyes. "Even a tall, dark, devilishly handsome doctor?"

"Especially a dark, devilish doctor," Colleen stated with more confidence than she felt.

Deidre smiled and gave her another hug. "I'm so glad you're here," she whispered near Colleen's ear. Colleen closed her eyes, sadness and worry filling her when she felt how desperately Deidre clung on to her…how much of her typically indomitable sister's rib cage she could feel through the cotton of her T-shirt.

"I can see the first thing I need to do is cook you a decent meal," Colleen told her when they broke apart, still holding hands.

Deidre waved her hand dismissively. "Linc's chef, Sasha, is terrific. My appetite has been off a bit since I came from Germany."

"Her appetite has been nonexistent," someone said in a blunt tone.

Colleen started when a tall man with chestnut-colored hair suddenly stepped into the foyer. He had a bold, handsome face and a powerful, rangy build. She noticed the way his gray-eyed, cool gaze landed on her sister's face. Deidre's back straightened, her chin went up and her eyes turned every bit as flinty as the man's.

"Nick Malone, I presume?" Colleen murmured wryly under her breath. Neither the man nor Deidre corrected her—just continued their staring duel—so Colleen knew she'd been right in her guess that the man was Lincoln DuBois's right-hand man and CEO of DuBois Enterprises—not to mention the man who made it clear he was suspicious of Deidre's motives in claiming to be Lincoln's daughter. Malone was younger and a heck of a lot better looking than she'd expected, but Deidre's haughty stance said loud and clear they were in the presence of the enemy.

"That's right," Deidre said. "Nick, I'd like you to meet my sister Colleen. Colleen, Nick Malone. She's come for the funeral." Deidre gave Colleen a bland glance. "Knowing Nick, he thinks you came to help me steal the silver, so I just thought I'd clarify."

Colleen suppressed a snort of laughter, but Nick's expression grew even harder at Deidre's jibe. Despite his jeans and Western-style shirt, Malone reminded Colleen more of a soldier than a cowboy or executive.

As usual, Deidre was fearless in the face of potential danger. She grabbed Colleen's free hand and pulled.

"Come on. We'd better get moving. Nick is likely to go into interrogation mode any second."

Colleen glanced at Nick bemusedly as they passed, but his gaze was glued to Deidre. Was that concern she saw on his face, mingling with annoyance? For some reason, the way he looked as he followed Deidre's retreating figure reminded her of the way Eric glared at her sometimes when she was being stubborn.

Chapter Thirteen

A painful stitch stabbed at Colleen's side as she and Deidre raced through the Holy Name parking lot, both of them wearing heels and holding hands to improve their balance. Their flight from Reno to Detroit had been delayed four hours because of weather, and now they were running late for Liam's and Natalie's dress rehearsal. Brigit had gone ahead and brought the kids with her to the wedding rehearsal, while Deidre and Colleen hurried to get ready.

Everything in the past twenty-four hours had happened so suddenly, it still felt a little surreal to her. She couldn't believe she was rushing to Liam's rehearsal dinner with Deidre in tow. They'd decided to surprise Brigit, Liam and Marc with Deidre's presence. Colleen didn't like to think about how either her mother or Deidre would act when they saw each other.

All of that was nerve-racking enough. But Colleen had to admit to herself that she was nervous and edgy because she was about to see Eric again. Would he be irritated at her for avoiding him all this time? Or would he be relieved? He'd stopped attempting to call her in the past week. Had he given up on trying to apologize for his intentions in seducing her? Was he ready to move on from the whole affair?

Dashing into the church vestibule, Deidre and she removed their coats and hung them on the rack in the entryway. In the distance, she heard Father Mike calling out instructions.

Her heart thrummed with dread and excitement as they entered the church. Deidre hadn't spoken to Brigit since she'd overheard an argument between Brigit and Derry sixteen years ago. In that argument, Derry had confronted Brigit with the fact that given their blood types, Deidre couldn't be his daughter. Brigit had admitted Derry wasn't Deidre's father, although she'd kept the identity of Deidre's biological father a secret until last summer.

Now Deidre was back in Harbor Town, and Colleen couldn't help but worry that all hell was going to break loose for the Kavanaughs—again.

Despite her worry about Deidre and Brigit, it was Eric's face she immediately sought out among the small crowd, not her mother's.

"Oh, my God," Deidre whispered without moving her lips. They paused at the back of the church, and the entire wedding party turned to look at them. "Is that Eric? He's gorgeous."

Colleen flushed, hoping fervently the excellent acoustics in the church hadn't made Deidre whisper carry. Deidre was indeed staring at Eric, and he did indeed look gorgeous, as usual. He wore a black suit, white shirt and pale tie. She hadn't been able to resist her sister's encouragements to reveal the truth about the reason for her frequent distractedness and occasional weepiness while they'd been in Tahoe. Now Deidre was privy to the secret workings of her heart. Well...most of them, anyway. There was no way she could convey with words the feelings she had seeing Eric at that moment.

The wedding party had apparently been practicing the bride's entrance, because Natalie was holding Eric's arm and they paused in the center aisle. His gaze fixed on her. Colleen couldn't interpret his expression. Her heart plummeted to the vicinity of her belly.

Suddenly, Liam gave a shout, and Marc, Mari, Liam and Natalie were converging on them at the back of the church.

"I can't believe it!" Liam said, laughing jubilantly as he hugged Deidre and picked her up, making her shriek in surprise. "You came!"

"I was wondering if I'd ever see the day," Marc said a moment later, beaming at Deidre. He gave her a big bear hug. When he glanced over Deidre's shoulder and saw Colleen standing there, smiling with joy, he reached and pulled her into the embrace. Laughing, Colleen put out an arm for Liam. The Kavanaugh children all engaged in a mutual, clumsy, heartfelt hug. "Do we owe you for this miracle?" Marc asked Colleen. "This is incredible."

"I'll say it is. All four of you together again in Harbor Town. I wondered if I'd ever see it again."

They all broke apart and turned at the sound of Brigit's voice. Brigit stared at her oldest daughter, her expression rapt. The hesitancy mingled with joy Colleen saw on her mother's face sent a pain through her heart.

"Deidre. You've made me so happy." She flew to her daughter, arms outstretched. Deidre didn't speak, just returned the hug, albeit stiffly. When they parted, Colleen saw a film of tears over Deidre's eyes, but she didn't allow one to spill.

Father Mike approached, greeting them enthusiastically. Everyone started talking. Colleen sighed in partial relief. She'd been dreading the moment, unsure of whether or not Deidre would turn a cold shoulder and cut Brigit completely. At least the initial greeting between mother and daughter had passed and gone tolerably well. Brendan and Jenny ran up to hug her. She'd missed them like crazy while she'd been in Tahoe and they'd stayed with their grandmother.

When she straightened, she realized that while everyone else conversed and made introductions, Eric was watching her with that dark-eyed, knowing look that always seemed to pierce right through her.

She licked her lower lip nervously. She should say hello, at least. No casual greeting seemed to fit the mixed anxiety, uncertainty and pleasure she experienced at seeing him again, though. He looked tense. Deidre had suggested—very delicately—while they'd been in Tahoe that Colleen may have been a tad defensive in not allowing Eric to fully explain himself. Was Deidre right? Was he angry? Concerned? Or was he completely immune to her now that he'd met his personal challenge of seducing her?

He took a step toward her, and her heart jumped into her throat.

"Okay, everyone, let's get back to business!" Father Mike called out, herding them back toward the front of the church.

Unfortunately, there was no opportunity for the next forty-five minutes to find out what Eric had been planning to say to her as Father Mike led them through the wedding proceedings. She kept stealing glances at him and occasionally caught him looking at her, but his expression gave her no clues as to what he was thinking or feeling. After they'd finished with rehearsal, she saw Natalie draw her brother aside and speak to him. Liam joined them. Eric nodded and approached Deidre. She became distracted when Brendan asked for permission for he and Jenny to ride to the restaurant with Eric.

"Eric wants us to," Brendan insisted when she demurred. "We're giving *Lucy* to Uncle Liam and Natalie after dinner tonight."

"*Lucy* is going to be in the parking lot, waiting for Natalie and Uncle Liam when they leave," Jenny said, brimming over with enthusiasm. Between the excitement of giving *Lucy* and the thrill of her flower-girl duties tomorrow, Colleen seriously doubted her girl would sleep well tonight.

A little later, she watched Eric leave with Brendan and Jenny. Everyone was trickling out of the church, leaving for the rehearsal dinner at Bistro Campagne.

"Natalie wants me to be in the wedding," Deidre said later as Colleen drove over to the restaurant.

"She does? That's a wonderful idea."

Deidre laughed. "I told her I couldn't. I don't have a dress to wear. But it was sweet of her to ask. I like her…and Eric, too. I can see what you meant about him. Tall, dark and smoldering. What eyes," Deidre added, giving Colleen a sideways, significant glance from the passenger seat.

She frowned, ignoring Deidre's mischievous expression.

"Is that what Eric was talking to you about? Being in the wedding?"

"In part," Deidre said lightly. "He also asked about you."

"He did?" she asked, nearly missing her turn. "What did he say?"

"He asked if you were doing all right. He said you looked pale. I told him he should ask you himself how you were. I said that all I knew was that you were up most nights in Tahoe, crying your eyes out."

"You *didn't*," Colleen declared in an ominous tone.

"Okay, I didn't," Deidre said, smiling angelically. "I'd never, you know that. I've got your back. Still…you guys should talk. I saw the way he was staring at you. If you seriously believe he was just interested in you for a challenge, you're nuts."

Colleen willed her breathing to calm and changed the subject. "Of course you should be in the wedding. You're Liam's sister. I have a dress you can wear. Mari and I chose our own dresses—we just made sure the colors and fabric matched in a general sense. I have another dark red dress you can borrow. I'll do some alterations on it tomorrow."

They chatted about the possibility until they entered Bistro Campagne and were shown to a reserved room. The wedding party was seated at the front of the room at a long table. Both Colleen and Natalie—who had also just arrived—insisted that Deidre sit at the head table. Colleen was chatting with Deidre and Mari when she noticed Eric enter the room with the kids. She waved at Jenny and Brendan as they sat down at a table with Brigit. Eric sat at the opposite end of the head table. Colleen watched him unobtrusively as he talked and joked with Marc.

"Colleen, did you have a chance to come up with something for your speech for the toast?" Mari asked her in a confidential tone.

She stared at Mari in horror. *Oh my God,* the toast. They'd agreed that Marc and Mari, as best man and matron of honor, would give the toast at the wedding reception, but Eric and Colleen were responsible for the rehearsal dinner traditional toasts to the bride and groom.

Deidre noticed her horrified expression. "What's wrong?"

"I thought there was a chance you'd forgotten, with everything going on, and you being away." Mari glanced at Deidre. "She's supposed to give the toast tonight."

Colleen took a large gulp of water. How could she have forgotten?

"Why don't you let me do it?" Deidre offered blithely.

"You wouldn't mind winging it?" Colleen asked in amazement as a waiter filled their champagne glasses. Most of the guests were seated now.

Deidre winked. "You're talking to an army nurse, remember? Making do with what I've got and winging it are my specialties."

She was relieved to pass the duty on to Deidre. Colleen was used to public speaking engagements for The Family

Center, but she liked to have something prepared. The sound of silver tinkling on crystal rung out, and the guests ceased their chatter. Eric stood to make his toast. Colleen was glad to have a valid excuse to stare at him.

"I was given the singular privilege tonight to toast the future happiness of this special couple, Liam and Natalie. I suppose I'm not the typical brother of the bride. I've also had the honor to be a father figure to Natalie and to watch her grow into the amazing young woman you see before you today."

Colleen found Eric's deep, resonant voice and striking good looks compelling, and she could tell by the many rapt faces in the room, she wasn't the only one.

"I won't lie to you and say that I didn't have my doubts when Natalie and Liam announced their engagement. I was cynical that anyone could be good enough for my little sister. She's one of the kindest people I know, generous to a fault. A braver soul never existed. There are things she's endured that would have broken me," he said, meeting Natalie's misty stare. He looked at Liam. "If you've won such a worthy heart, then you must deserve her. Is it possible for two people to fall so quickly for one another, to know with absolute, unquestionable certainty that this person is who they were meant to spend the rest of their lives with?" Colleen's heart skipped a beat when Eric's dark-eyed gaze landed on her and seemed to burn right down to her spirit. "Until recently, I would have said no. I would have denied cynicism and said I was just being rational in doubting the possibility of falling head over heels in love so fast, so completely. I would have said someone who claimed such a thing was not only foolish, but naive."

He paused, and Colleen held her breath.

"But tonight I gladly admit I was the one who was a naive fool for doubting. Love comes in many ways, if the trusting heart only lets it in." He raised his glass to the bride and groom. "Join me in toasting happiness and prosperity to a couple who taught this fool a measure of wisdom. To Natalie and Liam, may your brave, trusting hearts continue to beat strong and united for a lifetime."

"To Natalie and Liam," the guests murmured before they drank. Eric sat down to enthusiastic applause. The guests demanded a kiss by tinkling their goblets, which Liam and Natalie gladly provided.

"Great, how am I going to follow such a terrific toast?" Deidre grumbled. She did a double take when she glanced at Colleen's face. She smiled fondly and dried off Colleen's cheeks with her napkin. "I told you he wasn't just interested in a challenge."

Colleen sniffed and leaned forward, glancing down the table, only to see that Eric was doing the same toward her. While she hadn't been able to read him at all earlier, currently he was an open book. His expression was a little pained, as though he entreated for her understanding.

Maybe it was just the lighting, or maybe it was wishful thinking, but there was something in his dark eyes that looked a lot like love. She recalled his speech.

Love comes in many ways, if the trusting heart only lets it in.

He smiled. She beamed back at him.

It really was amazing, the way they could read each other's minds at times.

An hour and a half later, Colleen caught Eric's gaze and he gave a small nod. She entered the restaurant again and found a quiet, deserted hallway. The entire party had gone out into the parking lot to witness Liam and Natalie's reactions to *Lucy*. Eric, Brigit, Brendan and Jenny had done an amazing job. *Lucy* was perched on a trailer, awaiting her new owners, looking shiny and grand, and decked out in festive lights and a banner with Liam and Natalie's names. Brendan and Jenny were practically bursting with pride. Luckily, the photographer caught some excellent photos of Liam's and Natalie's disbelieving, ecstatic expressions when they realized the beautiful antique speedboat was theirs.

Colleen paused in the dim hallway, her heart beating more rapidly by the second. It swelled against her breastbone when she caught sight of Eric approaching her a few seconds later.

"You outdid yourself with *Lucy,*" she said quietly when he approached and stood before her, looking somber.

"Natalie and Liam seemed happy with her."

"Of course. They're ecstatic," Colleen murmured. The last thing she wanted was to have a casual conversation with him, but she was having difficulty finding the words. She started when he reached out and touched her cheek. Their gazes met.

"I'm sorry," he said.

"No. I'm sorry," she said in a rush. "I'm the one who got so defensive."

"I said it all wrong that afternoon."

"You said it very right tonight, during the toast."

"I meant it, every word. You, more than anything, changed my mind about the possibility of falling so hard and fast," he murmured. He moved his hand and stroked her hair, making her scalp tingle with excitement. He stepped closer, and Colleen breathed in his scent. Tears burned her eyelids at the familiar, cherished smell of clean skin, spice and Eric.

"That day when I dropped you off, I was only trying to tell you that I felt guilty for my original intention, where you were concerned. The way I feel about you now is nothing like what I felt then. It's true, I initially was interested in you for more...surface reasons, but that doesn't mean a guy can't change his mind, does it?"

"No. It doesn't."

He placed his hands on both sides of her jaw. "I would never hurt you," he said with fervent solemnity. "I want to spend the rest of my life with you. I promise I'll be faithful."

She shook her head, and tears spilled out of her eyes. How had he known that this was at the very heart of her doubt and fear?

"I believe you," she said, meaning it with all her heart.

"I love you," he said intently next to her mouth. "I love your kids. I love the whole package. Tell me what you said in the car the other day was true."

"I said a good many things I wish you'd forget," Colleen said in a trembling voice, "but if you mean the part where I said I'd fallen in love with you, that part couldn't have been truer."

His grin managed to be tender and triumphant at once. Colleen sighed when he pressed his long, hard body against hers. "I've been falling in love with you ever since Brendan's surgery. No...since Sunset Beach, even if I didn't recognize the symptoms then. If you'd have let me near you, I probably would have begun this delicate procedure a long time ago."

Colleen laughed, and more tears of happiness spilled down her cheeks, wetting his fingers. "That would have been far too easy."

"Maybe so," he said quietly, his mouth just inches from hers. "Our way of doing things was pretty damn perfect."

"At least it wasn't a boring romance," she whispered, brushing her lips against his.

"Life with you is never going to be boring," Eric muttered before he dipped his head, claiming Colleen utterly and completely with a searing kiss.

* * * * *

*Don't miss Deidre Kavanaugh's story,
the next book in
Beth Kery's* HOME TO HARBOR TOWN *miniseries
Coming soon to Harlequin Special Edition*

HEART & HOME

Heartwarming romances where love can
happen right when you least expect it.

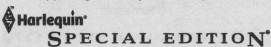

REQUEST YOUR FREE BOOKS!

2 FREE NOVELS PLUS 2 FREE GIFTS!

Harlequin

SPECIAL EDITION

Life, Love & Family

PRESENTING...

More Than Words

STORIES OF THE HEART

Three bestselling authors
Three real-life heroines

Even as you read these words, there are women just like you stepping up and making a difference in their communities, making our world a better place to live. Three such exceptional women have been selected as recipients of Harlequin's More Than Words award. To celebrate their accomplishments, three bestselling authors have written short stories inspired by these real-life heroines.

Proceeds from the sale of this book will be reinvested into the Harlequin More Than Words program to support causes that are of concern to women.

Visit

www.HarlequinMoreThanWords.com

to nominate a real-life heroine from your community.

Taft Bowman knew he'd ruined any chance he'd had for happiness with Laura Pendleton when he drove her away years ago…and into the arms of another man, thousands of miles away. Now she was back, a widow with two small children…and despite himself, he was starting to believe in second chances.

Harlequin Special® Edition® presents a new installment in USA TODAY *bestselling author RaeAnne Thayne's miniseries,* THE COWBOYS OF COLD CREEK.

Enjoy a sneak peek of A COLD CREEK REUNION

Available April 2012 from Harlequin® Special Edition®

A younger woman stood there, and from this distance he had only a strange impression, as though she was somehow standing on an island of calm amid the chaos of the scene, the flashing lights of the emergency vehicles, shouts between his crew members, the excited buzz of the crowd.

And then the woman turned and he just about tripped over a snaking fire hose somebody shouldn't have left there.

Laura.

He froze, and for the first time in fifteen years as a firefighter, he forgot about the incident, his mission, just what the hell he was doing here.

Laura.

Ten years. He hadn't seen her in all that time, since the week before their wedding when she had given him back his ring and left town. Not just town. She had left the whole damn country, as if she couldn't run far enough to get away from him.

Some part of him desperately wanted to think he had made some kind of mistake. It couldn't be her. That was just some other slender woman with a long sweep of honey-blond hair and big, blue, unforgettable eyes. But no. It was definitely Laura. Sweet and lovely.

Not his.

He was going to have to go over there and talk to her. He didn't want to. He wanted to stand there and pretend he hadn't seen her. But he was the fire chief. He couldn't hide out just because he had a painful history with the daughter of the property owner.

Sometimes he hated his job.

Will Taft and Laura be able to make the years recede...or is the gulf between them too broad to ever cross?

Find out in
A COLD CREEK REUNION
Available April 2012 from Harlequin® Special Edition®
wherever books are sold.

Celebrate the 30th anniversary
of Harlequin® Special Edition® with a bonus story
included in each Special Edition® book in April!

**Get swept away with a brand-new miniseries
by USA TODAY bestselling author**

MARGARET WAY

The Langdon Dynasty

Amelia Norton knows that in order to embrace her future,
she must first face her past. As she unravels her family's secrets,
she is forced to turn to gorgeous cattleman Dev Langdon for
support—the man she vowed never to fall for again.

Against the haze of the sweltering Australian heat Mel's
guarded exterior begins to crumble...and Dev will do
whatever it takes to convince his childhood sweetheart
to be his bride.

THE CATTLE KING'S BRIDE
Available April 2012

And look for
ARGENTINIAN IN THE OUTBACK
Coming in May 2012